JUAN PABLO
AND
THE
BUTTERFLIES

JUAN PABLO

AND

THE

BUTTERFLIES

JJ Flowers

Merit Press

New York   London   Toronto   Sydney   New Delhi

ℳeritPress

Merit Press
An Imprint of Simon & Schuster, Inc.
1230 Avenue of the Americas
New York, NY 10020

First Merit Press hardcover edition MAY 2017

MERIT PRESS and colophon are trademarks of Simon and Schuster.

For information about special discounts for bulk purchases, please contact Simon & Schuster Special Sales at 1-866-506-1949 or business@simonandschuster.com.

The Simon & Schuster Speakers Bureau can bring authors to your live event. For more information or to book an event contact the Simon & Schuster Speakers Bureau at 1-866-248-3049 or visit our website at www.simonspeakers.com.

Interior design by Sylvia McArdle

Interior images © 123RF/melpomen

Manufactured in the United States of America

10 9 8 7 6 5 4 3 2 1

Library of Congress Cataloging-in-Publication Data has been applied for.

ISBN 978-1-5072-0214-2
ISBN 978-1-5072-0215-9 (ebook)

DEDICATION

This novel is dedicated to:
Beethoven,
John and Jonpaul, the two brightest lights in my life,
everyone who has lost a loved one,
and to the refugee and migrant children of the world.
May the light lead you home.
For the butterflies . . .

CHAPTER ONE

Machine-gun fire!

Juan Pablo cracked open the door of his modest home and peered down the darkened street. The *bratatat* sounded louder than the blaring music and a furious rev of engines. Like a hammer to glass, the onslaught of noise destroyed the quiet of the butterfly sanctuary. Headlights swept El Rosario's plaza as several trucks and an SUV circled the cobblestone square. Armed men hung off the side of the trucks and the relentless barrage of their machine guns filled the star-filled night.

Narco-traffickers. Here in El Rosario, home to a billion monarch butterflies and the two dozen families who loved them.

Juan Pablo slammed the brightly painted front door with the rainbow-colored WELCOME! sign. For the first time in his life, he found the rusty old lock and bolted it. He rushed to switch off the lamp at his abuela's bedside before collapsing to the floor. He finished his ninth desperate text to the *Novedades de México*, the major newspaper for Mexico City.

Help! Narco-traffickers are shooting up the plaza in El Rosario. No one is left but our neighbors Mario and Rocio Ruiz and my abuela, Dr. Elena Venesa. She is unconscious with a fever—we need a doctor. Please send help.

After hitting send, he texted Rocio, who was hiding in the cantina:

Juan Pablo: *They're here.*
Rocio: *Outside.*

Juan Pablo: *Can u get here?*
Rocio: *Too late. Under the bed. Scared. Praying. You? Elena?*
Juan Pablo: *Same. She is so still.*
Rocio: *Abuelo will request an ambulance for her.*
Juan Pablo: *Be safe, Rocio. Don't come out until they are gone. Promise me.*
Rocio: *I promise.*

Juan Pablo stared with horror at his shaking hands. His violinist's fingers, long, calloused, agile, and strong, had never failed him before. He clasped them tight, and made his way to the door to listen.

Last week a large black, red, and white banner sporting a menacing el diablo with sinister eyes and a leering grin stretched across the sole road into their sleepy town. This was how the drug cartel marked a territory and warned the people that the police could not protect them now. The tourists had departed with most of the butterflies nearly a month before. Of the locals, everyone with relatives in Mexico City, Guadalajara, or anywhere with a larger population and so somewhat safer, had packed up and left. Everyone promised to send help back to save the old lady they all loved, but no help ever came. No ambulance dared pass these murderous gangs.

Machine-gun fire cracked like thunder and lightning into the sky. Would Rocio be safe under the bed?

Born auspiciously one year, one month, one day apart from him, Rocio was his best friend in this life. (Even though she was bossy and they spent half the time arguing with each other, *like two puppies roughhousing,* his abuela said more than once. *You, Juan Pablo, such a know-it-all, and Rocio, always so bossy, this great cosmic dance between you two is hilarious already . . .*) He closed his eyes, conjuring Rocio's waist-length dark hair and bright, teasing eyes, her skinny legs, and big feet.

Rocio's uncle in La Peñita de Jaltemba, just north of Puerto Vallarta, begged them to leave before it was too late, but both Mario and Rocio had refused. They would not leave either him or his abuela. "Even if my abuelo could bear to lose the cantina to the banditos, how could we possibly leave Elena and you, JP?"

Mario had agreed with his granddaughter. "Elena saved my beautiful wife's life. She saw my daughter into this world and then Leonardo and Rocio. She taught Leonardo all she knows about the herbs and potions and helped him become a doctor too, bless her." Rocio's mother worked as a nurse in Arizona, helping to pay for Leonardo's medical school in Puerto Rico and she was now very close to becoming a U.S. citizen. "We owe everything to Elena; we all do," Mario added. "Besides, Rocio would never forgive me if anything happened to you, Juan Pablo."

You could sometimes reason with these modern-day monsters, Mario had heard. Wasn't it rumored that they sometimes paved a road or built a school or gave money to an orphanage? Mario planned to beg them to let an ambulance through for an old woman. "We will pay whatever they ask. Even the worse banditos would not let an abuela die for no good reason. And since no one is here but us and the butterflies, they will soon tire of El Rosario and be gone."

Juan Pablo's hands combed back his long hair, as if this would help him think. Just keep Rocio safe—that's all he knew. They wouldn't hurt her, would they?

She was just a girl, only fourteen.

The relentless gunfire and booming music snatched the hope, replacing it with an escalating fear as Juan Pablo thought of the hundreds of stories of the narco-traffickers' brutality and viciousness. *Like a deadly virus consuming my beloved country.* His abuela had shaken her head helplessly, knowing of no medicine or magic with which to save Mexico from this terrible plague. Everyone had at least one relative, often more, who had lost their life's savings, died, disappeared, or lived in fear of dying and disappearing. This army of the devil shot people for no reason anyone knew, and like demons from hell, they often tortured them first. They were known to disappear whole families, killing those police that they couldn't bribe, and taking over whole towns before stealing everyone's money. They recruited boys even younger than him, forcing them to rob, hide drugs, kill, or be killed. His abuela always imagined El Rosario, their tiny portion of paradise, was at least safe, that the mountains and the butterflies themselves would always protect them. But this was not so anymore.

The gunfire and rev of engines abruptly ceased.

Unlatching the rusty lock, Juan Pablo cautiously cracked the door an inch in order to better hear. A man shouted orders, his loud demands rising above the noise of drunken laughter. Tajo, Rocio's dog, barked frantically at the commotion.

Gunfire sounded again, followed by Tajo's surprised yelp.

"No, no. Dios mío," Mario cried out, this barely audible. "Tajo. Tajo."

Juan Pablo's brows drew a sharp line above his green eyes.

Did they shoot Tajo? Why would they shoot a little dog?

Sweet, friendly Tajo, their town's mascot. Tajo, whose wagging tail greeted the tourist buses, who followed them up to the meadow in the afternoons. Tajo, who loved his violin's music, Mario's leftover uchepos, and Rocio's gentle hands. If they killed a small dog, what else could they do? Would they let an ambulance through to aid an old lady? Would they leave a young girl unharmed?

The answer ricocheted through his mind, but how could he stop them? He was just a teenager, tall maybe, but skinny too. He had no gun, power, and worse, no courage. He might love superheroes, but he was not one of them. All he knew was music and books; he was the exact opposite of an action hero.

He shut the door again, bolting it again.

His gaze found his abuela's still form on the small cot. How could the old woman fall ill now, when they needed her most?

His abuela was both a real doctor and the local curandera. The old ways had been passed down to her and after absorbing this ancient wisdom, she had gone on to attend Mexico City's medical school. She had wanted to make sure she knew every aspect of healing.

Still, it was the old woman's shamanic powers that were a good deal more popular than her famous doctoring skill. Nothing made his abuela happier than taking away people's aches and pains, their troubles and struggles. She took away the pain of childbirth as well as the opposite, the struggle of transitioning. She cured little Jose's poor hearing, but also his mother's gambling problem, Ms. Sanchez's strange rash, but also her husband's infidelity, Mr. Hernandez's high blood pressure, but also his depression. Occasionally she worked miracles, curing dementia, diabetes, and even many different cancers. People sought her out from hundreds of miles away.

Now, of all times, for the very first time, she was the one who needed help.

The old woman might imagine she was connected to the spirit realm, but if he could not get her to a hospital, she would be living in this strange and magical place, a place the old woman maintained was as real as life on earth. Life, all of it, according to his abuela, was a manifestation of the spiritual; when the body died, the soul shot straight to the spiritual realm to become one with the Sky People.

Who are the Sky People? he must have first asked long ago, realizing his abuela felt a connection to people he did not see.

You once lived in the sky, Juan Pablo. Don't you remember? When he shook his head, he received a *tsk, tsk,* finished with a smile. *Now you live in this skin bound to the earth. But all the souls that love you, and there are more of them than you will ever know here, live in the sky.*

Who, Abuela?

Well, for instance, your mother, Julieta. Your other abuelos and their parents. The souls of everyone who has ever lived. The Sky People.

Like Rocio's heaven and angels?

People who think of heaven don't realize that the spiritual realm and our material world on earth are not separated by death, but rather they interact with each other in powerful, important ways. The two realms act more as mirrors reflecting each other . . . The closer you are to the Sky People, the more the separation blurs.

Still later, as doubts grew with his age, he finally said, *Scientists would say the Sky People live only in your imagination.*

Ah, she nodded. *This is true. The imagination is how the Sky People talk to us.*

Pacing now, he covered his ears to escape the distant drum of the ugly music. Before this invasión, his biggest problem had been finding good Wi-Fi for his violin lessons, perfecting Bach's Allegro, and whether he should read the last Harry Potter book in his beloved Spanish or in the sometimes more difficult English.

Seeking the old woman's familiar comfort, he approached the cot and stared down at her small brown head peeking out from her favorite orange blanket. The blanket formed the shape of a colorful kite, her long gray braid its tail, as if waiting for a wind to carry her up.

For several minutes, he closed his eyes, willing her to wake.

"Juan Pablo."

His eyes flew open to the miracle. The old woman's soft brown eyes stared back. "Abuela, you're awake! You've been asleep so long . . ."

She shook her head and closed her eyes again as if pained. "It is time."

"Time?" he repeated before starting to explain the dangerous siege taking place outside their door.

She stopped him with a slight shake of her head. "It is time for you to make the journey north. To follow the butterflies."

"Follow the butterflies? North?"

"Sí, to America."

He tried to make sense of this, but couldn't. Her illness must be speaking.

"Take your violin, of course, and the seeds. Use them to make your way."

The townspeople sold packets of milkweed seeds to the tourists. Milkweed fed the butterflies on their perilous journey from El Rosario to the great lands of North America. It took four generations of butterflies traveling 4,200 kilometers to make the mystical pilgrimage, a journey that ended with their return to the ancient forested mountains of Sierra Madre. Tourists came to their small town from all over America to see the millions of winged creatures together in one magical place. During the winter months, as the butterflies' numbers grew and grew, these winged creatures swallowed up the whole of the blue sky. Other times they appeared as a colorful stream riding an invisible river of wind above. The delicate beings clustered so thick on the trees, it was not uncommon for branches to break off, sending thousands of orange and black butterflies into the air with a cacophony of sound and color.

The butterflies sustained the people of El Rosario.

"Be generous with our seeds," his abuela continued, unaware of the emergency just down the street in the square, or even her grandson's desperation. "And always follow the butterflies' path; they will not steer you wrong."

He glanced anxiously at the door, as if the banditos might be bursting through any minute.

"Cross the Sea of Cortez to Baja, and continue north. I think you should pass over the invisible line separating our two lands in

Tijuana. This might be difficult, but you are clever. You will find a way. Follow the ocean's shore north, just like our butterflies."

All he could think of was getting the idea out of her mind. "Abuela, you don't understand. Banditos, here, in Rosario—"

Yet the old woman was not listening. She reached for his hand, as if needing more of his wide-eyed attention. "To save a life and slay a beast. This is your journey, your transformación. Promise me," she said with sudden intensity before she remembered. "You must reach Pacific Grove before summer's end. In August, late August . . ."

Pacific Grove? This was another butterfly sanctuary, he knew, but one far away in California, the golden land of dreams: Hollywood, Apple, Google, Facebook, Twitter, and Disneyland. (Since they were small, he and Rocio dreamed of visiting the Magic Kingdom, and sometimes he could even cajole Rocio into pretending they were in Disneyland.) There was also the Golden Gate Bridge that spanned the beautiful city by the bay. Beyond San Francisco stretched the land of the magnificent redwoods, trees taller than the tallest buildings. (His abuela had always dreamed of touching a redwood tree in the north and "looking up to see how small I am.") California, this golden land, more than a thousand miles away, but might as well be a million miles away, for he could never reach it. He had no car, no money, and most of all, no papers.

"Promise me," she demanded again.

"Sí, sí," he had finally relented to ease her worry, stealing another anxious glance at the door.

"Remember, the Sky People will always be with you . . ."

A large butterfly floated in from the tiny kitchen off to the side.

He stared in wonder at the miracle as the winged creature drew close and began circling his abuela's cot.

The wrinkled face changed with a smile, despite her illness and fever, and a twinkle lit her strange amber eyes. "A good omen, that."

"Impossible . . ." Juan Pablo managed the single word.

Butterflies cannot fly at night. The sun fueled their flight. Without the warmth of the sun, there could be no flying.

Butterflies, according to his abuela, were the living symbols of spirit energy in the material world, a reminder to all souls of a transcendent purpose.

He watched as the butterfly floated out of sight again. Never, in all his life, had he seen a butterfly fly at night.

He was about to give it chase, to set it safely in a tree, but his abuela's eyes closed again and she muttered her last words, the strangest of all. "He will be waiting for you in the sanctuary at Pacific Grove, Juan Pablo."

"Quién, Abuela? Who will be waiting for me?"

She sounded far away. "I see it Juan Pablo. I will be there, too, listening when you play. All the Sky People will be listening."

"Abuela, you cannot go. We cannot go . . ."

Yet, just like that, she went very still, lifeless once more.

They needed an ambulance to get her to the hospital. The old lady was all he had in this world.

She was exactly half of what he loved. The other half was made up of music, the butterflies, and Rocio. Every year fewer of the colorful winged creatures returned to El Rosario, and this year, in alarmingly diminished numbers, they had left for North America early. That his abuela would begin fading with the butterflies seemed like a coincidence, but she always said coincidences were no more than an awakening to the miracle of life.

Dropping to the floor, he hung his head helplessly between his knees.

Clear as stars in a cloudless night sky, a voice sounded in his mind, "Save Rocio."

His head shot up and he scrambled to his feet. "Abuela?"

The slightest rise of her chest triggered a relieved gasp.

He was going loco. He must have only imagined those words. He did not have to wonder why. Rocio might not be safe if these banditos found her. He found his iPad:

JP: *Are you okay?*

As he waited for Rocio's response, and the seconds ticked off, his tension mounted. He stared at the screen until it blurred. He needed to get Rocio back here. They would lock the door and keep the lights off, hiding until the banditos left.

He thought of the superheroes he loved: Spider-Man, Batman, Harry Potter. They knew fear, but ignored it. Fear never stopped them from acting. Nothing that could happen to him would be worse than someone hurting Rocio.

Moving to the door, he slowly opened it again. Men's voices rose against the screaming backdrop of shrieking music. The booming, rhythmic thud of their music was worse than the machine-gun fire to his sensitive ears. The cars were parked strategically between the Cantina where Rocio hid in the family's apartment above, Carlos's souvenir shop, the café, and the petro station.

Their cottage was very last on the street before the landscape opened up to the forest sanctuary of the mountain. Normally, at this hour, every home would have been bustling with the familiar noise of families having dinner, making music, playing games, or just watching TV. Now the streets appeared dark and deserted, like a ghost town. The strange quiet produced an unnatural stillness, but one that ended in sudden chaos at the cantina.

He would just sneak up to see what they were about. To make sure Rocio stayed safe.

Returning to his abuela's bedside, he hurriedly brushed his lips to her forehead. "Keep fighting, Abuela. Be strong. I will be right back," he promised, even though he suspected she no longer heard the words of this world.

A quarter moon rose in the night sky. Nearby, the orange point of Mars hung in the velvet space, all of it surrounded by a thousand tiny pinpoints of light. The air felt mild for spring, poised on the edge of summer's warming. He quietly shut the door before slipping into the darkness.

He kept to the sides of the modest homes lining the cobblestone street, moving cautiously, stealthily toward the plaza. If only he had Harry Potter's invisibility cloak. His curly dark hair, dark jeans, and black sweatshirt and sneakers blended into the shadows, but anyone looking might spot him.

Only the bass of the banditos' music interrupted the eerie quiet. He reached the last house before the shops began. Normally the bright yellow adobe house boomed with the boisterous noise of three generations of Rodriguezes, but now stood as still and dark as Espy's café and bakery tucked alongside the petro station in the plaza. The restaurant sign for Florendo's Ts—the cantina's only competition in town—hung lifeless over the patio. Juan Pablo could barely make out the outrageous claims in the dim light: *Voted best Tortillas, Tacos, and Tequila in Mexico*. Mario was alternatively amused and infuriated by his competition's blatant exagerando. The chairs and tables were piled up six feet in a corner, covered in canvas in case of rain.

He made no sound as he continued to the petro station.

Juan Pablo slipped behind the side of the building and pressed against the wall, hidden in the shadows. The station's lights were off, and the little store inside was closed and locked, despite the now empty shelves. He started past the restrooms and as he did so, his foot brushed a strange, unfamiliar lump. He stumbled, washed in a hot panic as he righted himself. For several tense moments he held perfectly still, understanding the English metaphor *frozen with fear* for the first time.

Collecting his wits, his gaze finally fell to his feet to ascertain what the small lump was.

Tajo's body. Poor, poor brave Tajo.

They shot him dead. Why would they kill a little dog? If they would snatch such a small life for no good reason, what might they do to the rest of them?

Terrifying images answered the question.

Save Rocio. Nothing else mattered.

The music's volume rose suddenly. Like an alarm bell, he forced himself to move. He at last came to the other side of the building, now close enough to see.

Men gathered in front of a truck, passing a bottle of tequila and two odd-shaped pipes between themselves. Machine guns hung recklessly from their shoulders. Rows of shiny bullets belted their waists. Laughter erupted but he couldn't make out the words beneath the blaring song "Cuerno de Chivo," or "Goat's Horn," an awful song about the love for a rifle.

This was not his beloved Beethoven or Bach or Haydn.

The Torres family had left Mario a gun, Rocio had told him. Just in case, but what folly that seemed now.

One man, one gun against a dozen machine guns.

A man, his skin darkened with tattoos, mentioned the foco wearing off and needing more. "First," he managed before a wheezing inhale, "Alimenta a la máquina." *Feed the machine.*

"Mas? You loco, Rencor," another laughed, as he took the cigarette.

The last year he went to school, before he and Rocio started at the online Khan Academy, Juan Pablo's teacher had shown a slide show about the dangers of this drug called foco. English translation: crystal meth. People became hyped up and crazy as it first stole your good sense, next your money and morals, and finally, your teeth. His teacher said people who were addicted to foco had been known to murder in order to get high.

Juan Pablo had asked his abuela *Why? Why did people choose this craziness?*

There are many reasons, but they all stem from people becoming separated from love. People find themselves sad and without hope. Futures without hope are empty places, frightening because of it. These drugs appear on their paths, and like all material things, as an illusion of happiness. Desperate, they grab them and cling greedily. But soon they discover the chimera has been replaced by an ever-widening pit of despair and misery. A very few find the strength to climb back to the light, but most of these poor souls fall into the darkness.

They looked like any gathering of friends on a street corner after a long day's work. Perfectly ordinary, except for the tattoos and guns slung over their shoulders. And the shiny gold jewelry hanging from tattooed necks, the diamonds decorating their fingers. Still, they all wore a uniform of black pants or jeans and red or black shirts or sleeveless white T-shirts.

Nature pairs black and red to warn us, he remembered his abuela once said to Leonardo, who she had many years tutored in herbs and medicines to prepare him for medical school. *Whenever you see it, be careful . . .*

He abruptly found himself staring at the shortest man. Stocky and muscular, he wore only a vest, as if to show off his physique. In other circumstances Rocio, he knew, would have made fun of such a person. *Look at my muscles,* she would pretend to preen. *I am Mr. Peacock.* He and Rocio would have laughed at this fun.

Ropes of various lengths hung from his belt like trophies. A shorter gold one stood out against the black pants, but what the heck was it?

Another group of men sat at a table on the cantina's patio. An enormous man stood protectively behind them with his ear to a phone. Probably a bodyguard, the way his gaze swept the area, as if his eyes refused to settle on any one thing. A loose-fitting black dress shirt over black trousers draped his massive shape. A bear housed in human form. He had a large round head, as bald as a soccer ball, and almost as big. His puffy face squeezed his small, dark eyes. It was impossible to imagine this man smiling.

The festive lanterns strung across the patio looked out of place.

He needed to get closer.

A simple plan formed in his mind. As soon as the banditos left or fell asleep, he would find Rocio under the bed and escort her to their hideout in the meadow. Even if the men found him and his abuela, Rocio would be safe there.

It was not a good plan, but it was the best he could do for now.

Juan Pablo slipped quietly around the back of the gas station. He came around the other side, close enough to hear the words of the men gathered at the truck. Laughter and smoke and the horrible music greeted him, the assaults of sounds no louder than the furious thud of his heart.

At first he thought they talked about braids, how there would be no more or trophies from this ghost town. They used coarse words for women.

Braids, trophies . . . Juan Pablo's gaze returned to the ropes hanging from the Peacock's belt.

These were not ropes, but hair. Girl's braided hair. Just like ill-fated animals' heads on a trophy hunter's wall, no girl had willingly parted with her braids.

He thought of Rocio's long hair.

He sucked in his next breath with the terror of it.

Get Rocio out of here.

Memories flooded his consciousness, warning him of the stakes here.

Almost every day he and Rocio hiked to the meadow blooming with a million golden creatures searching for a place in the sun. He'd play the piece he was learning while Rocio danced around him, butterflies decorating the dark hair like living flowers. The girl flew round and round, Rocio's laughter singing with the music.

They learned how to stop time with their joy.

Following his abuela's suggestion, he and Rocio had built an Indian tepee in the forest just beyond the meadow. No one else but his abuela knew about it. The tepee became their secret, a private tent where they passed the endless hours of childhood playing imaginary games: Indians—Rocio was the chief and he was the brave; hospital—Rocio was the doctor and he the patient; school—Rocio was the teacher and he the student; and the Hogwarts School of Witchcraft and Wizardry—finally, he was Harry Potter and Rocio was Hermione. But lately, as they began outgrowing imaginary games, they hiked up to the tepee just to read good books like *The Adventures of Huckleberry Finn* and *The Old Man and the Sea*, but also *The Fault in Our Stars* and *The Hunger Games*. For these interruptions of their normal life, they had begun to abandon their constant arguing, and simply lay side to side and head to head. Without ever speaking of it, they both understood that something new had slipped between them, something that waited like the butterflies for the sun . . .

He released his breath all at once, tense with a rising dread.

They would soon leave, he told himself. Rocio was hidden and safe. No one would find her.

The giant bodyguard bent over and whispered to a man at the table. This man must be el amo de la droga, the boss. He wore a gray felt hat and leather vest over a black T-shirt. Weird pink sunglasses, perched on his nose, failed to hide his droopy eyes. Like he was half asleep and not too bright to begin with. The boss man held up a hand as he removed a phone from his pocket.

The music stopped. The other men fell silent.

"Amigo," he said into the phone after a minute. "Sí, this is Carlos . . . Ha! The legions of dead do not concern us." He chuckled. "We have the best químicos this side of the Rio Grande." Listening, he knocked back a shot of tequila.

Juan Pablo grasped the meaning of the man's words. The cartels were said to have huge vats of acid that destroy bodies, leaving no trace of a human being. Thousands upon thousands of people had disappeared this way.

The saddest thing is loved ones not knowing, his abuela had said. *Their hearts wage a battle between hope and grief, which eventually becomes the darkest despair.*

He cautiously peered out again.

The boss man Carlos wore a creepy smile, as if the smirk came with murderous thoughts. His abuela always said people's deeds were etched on their face. *Kindness is written there, but cruelty, too.* He now knew what she meant. The man's face spelled the word *mean*. Not a normal mean, but the kind of mean that was for no reason. English word: *malice.*

"Our crew will clean up when it is done," Carlos continued into his phone. "Armies disappear, trust me on this. That's right. You don't want to let us down. My brother has no patience these days. In fact he has hired . . . the Hunter"—he pronounced the word slowly, for emphasis—"to take out our garbage. Ah"—his smirk appeared again—"now you are afraid. Good. Then get it done." He returned his phone to the pocket.

Juan Pablo was surprised to see that the mention of the Hunter held the awesome power to, if not frighten, then agitate these men. "It is true?" the tattooed man Rencor asked. "Your brother has hired the Hunter?"

Carlos nodded in a pretense of indifference. "He has been useful to us lately. He took out those four Texas border agents who were stealing from us. Then, that new pandilla that was causing problems."

"Sí, when he has a reason," one of the men said, disgruntled. A fist-sized upside-down cross studded with diamonds hung over his black T-shirt, catching the light. "If the Hunter enjoyed killing, but no, he might be looking at you across a room, and boom."

"Sí, sí," the Peacock nodded, nervous or maybe excited, Juan Pablo couldn't tell. "Once at a party, he killed six people. Big customers, too. And afterward he just sat there, red boots resting on the table, smoking his cigarro."

"That was maldito loco." The tattooed man Rencor nodded. "No one had the balls to ask why?"

An odd-looking man sitting across from Carlos spoke next, his words seeming to have more weight than the others. "You can't trust him." Long hair was wrapped tightly on the crown of his head like an old woman, making his already long face seem even longer. A line-thin mustache sat above a small mouth. "La mitad de la raza." He spat on the patio. "I don't trust any Americano, even half-breeds like him."

Rencor nodded as he leaned toward Carlos. "One time Salvador sent the Hunter to clean up. It was a big job, so Salvador sent a crew of five with him. The Hunter said he didn't need help, but Salvador insisted, for safety. And then no one came back. Sí, the mess was no more, but neither was the crew." He locked gazes with his boss. "Remember, Carlos?"

Juan Pablo tried to imagine this Hunter, the man with the red boots, but he could not. How could there be a man worse than these men?

Even Carlos appeared uncomfortable with the subject. "He gets the job done. No questions. Finito, done, everyone is muerto; the problem is no more." He looked around, as if for a distraction, just as Mario appeared carrying a bottle of tequila.

Even Juan Pablo saw Mario's fear across the distance.

Which was what Carlos lasered in on. "Any mujer hiding here, old man?"

Mario's eyes widened. He shook his head. "No, no."

For a long minute Juan Pablo saw Mario through Carlos's predatory gaze. In his sixtieth decade, short and heavy, Mario was no match for even one of these men. The old man's large belly spoke of his easy life of few worries. *Rocio, your abuelo, bless his soul,* his abuela warned recently, as she concocted a potion for his bad knees and weak heart. *He needs to stop eating like a barn animal and start eating like a hummingbird or I fear even my medicine will fail.* Mario looked as soft and scared as an old rabbit caught in sight of circling hawks.

"Look at that." Carlos first smiled, but then took on a tone of disgust. "What kind of man cannot hide his fear?" He motioned to his bodyguard. "Dimi, search the apartment upstairs."

Dios mío. Juan Pablo pressed harder against the wall.

The giant man headed into the apartment above the cantina where Rocio hid.

Would he find her? Be still, Rocio. Hold very still . . .

Juan Pablo heard the elephant boots pounding up the stairs. Maddeningly, the rancorous talk of the men drowned out any more sound. Several tense moments passed, until—

Rocio's sudden scream electrified the air. The men fell silent for a minute. From upstairs a masculine grunt greeted the girl's terrified protests and the brief futile sounds of a scuffle. The clap of the boots going down.

The men erupted into collective laughter as the big man appeared with Rocio over his shoulder. Her fists still pounded his wide back, but she might have been hitting air for all the effect. He set her on her feet and stood behind her as if presenting a present. Rocio wore her favorite jeans and purple Winnie the Pooh T-shirt, a long-ago gift from a cousin who actually went to the Magic Kingdom. Her long hair fell in tangled disarray down her back, her bright eyes, changed with fear, looked out from beneath the sharp line made by her bangs. The big man's hands dug into her slim shoulders.

Seeing the men at the table, she shook her head slightly, listening to the crude comments her appearance solicited.

Gun pointing, Mario came out from the kitchen in protest, but stopped in an instant. As if conjured in a magician's trick, four guns pointed at Mario. The old man's gun fell with a loud clamor to the floor. He slowly held up his arms in surrender. A bandito rushed forward and claimed his gun.

"She is my nieta. She is only a girl."

"Ah, but she is a pretty little thing, no?"

"Ripe for the plucking . . ."

"Too young for my tastes," Carlos said, disappointment in his tone.

"But I love the virgins." This was muttered by the Peacock, and he waved one of the braids like a snake wagging its tongue.

Carlos laughed with his men at this. "That virginity is worth more than you make in a month, amigo."

"I will pay for it," he answered, cheerfully. "I am very good at breaking them in." Now he made a crude gesture with his hips.

"Hmm. Any other bids for the treat?"

Numbers were shouted in an obscene bidding war.

As if encouraged by his men's awful enthusiasm, Carlos's droopy eyes came to rest on the girl. "It looks as if I will first make sure this shiny piece is worth such a sum."

Juan Pablo felt dizzy with sickness.

Carlos snapped his fingers, ordering Rocio tied up.

The bodyguard laughed and tossed her over his shoulder again. Just like that, he carried Rocio away upstairs. The girl's fists pummeled his back and she kicked for all she was worth, but to no avail.

A loud buzzing filled Juan Pablo's ears, as if to block out the obscenities that followed this show.

"First, food, grandpa. Get some food out here pronto."

Mario stood in a terrified stupor of helplessness and desperation.

A gun fired close to Mario's feet.

He stumbled back into the kitchen. The men laughed uproariously.

With his heart pounding furiously, the queer ringing growing louder in his ears, Juan Pablo closed his eyes where he stood, trying to think of how to save her, the girl that he loved more than life itself.

The Sky People will always help you in a time of need, but you must always ask first.

Abuela, he had laughed, *how can the spirits help me? Help anyone? If they are made of light?*

O, many ways. If you just show them a problem, they will show you the solution.

But how?

It is different each time. Sometimes the answer appears in a dream. Or, a message. Often they will direct your mind to the solution that is right in front of you.

As he had grown older, Juan Pablo had gone through a period of doubting the reality of his abuela's Sky People and he had often teased her about them. *Abuela, why don't you ask the Sky People for a large-screen TV so we don't have to watch these science shows on my iPad.* His abuela loved science; she was a serious consumer of science programs.

O, Juan Pablo, for someone so smart, you are sometimes very foolish. I've told you a hundred times, the Sky People are not like a fairy godmother or Santa Claus. They don't answer wish lists like that . . . She became distracted by a bluebird perched on a sunflower outside the window. *Not usually anyway . . .*

Those last words, *not usually,* served as motivation to test the old woman's beliefs when Joshua Bell, the world's best violinist, came to Mexico City last year. Though he had nothing to lose, he felt as ridiculous as a kitten battling a pesky moth. Nothing happened at first, but then he hadn't really expected anything to happen. Then . . . three days later, someone, probably a rich American, left a $100 bill in his violin case as he played in the plaza for the tourists. This windfall had bought the best night of his and Rocio's life: a long bus ride to Mexico City, a wonderful dinner at the restaurant of one of Abuela's friends, and the performance of a lifetime. Since that nice bit of magic, he had asked the Sky People for help many times, but only, as his abuela advised, for guidance with music. He still wasn't completely sure he believed in his abuela's Sky People, but somehow, whether it was a trick of his mind or no, he did always receive help just when he needed it most.

He would never need help more than now.

Juan Pablo sent a furtive, frantic prayer to the Sky People for help. He imagined the earth cracking open up and swallowing these beasts, but no such thing happened.

Which is not to say nothing happened.

The speed with which help came was a shock; it landed like a hard blow to his head. From that moment on he never thought; he only acted.

Retracing his steps, he ran back to his house. He slipped through the door. The profound stillness in the room brought back the awareness of the powerful buzz in his ears. Like static, it felt like a cacophony urging him forward at a furious speed.

Wasting no time, he turned on his iPad's flashlight.

He placed the stepladder under the uppermost shelves. Carefully marked jars, all sizes, lined the shelves and it took several frantic minutes to find the right one. Gripping it tightly, he clicked off the light, jumped off the ladder and rushed from the room, never noticing the momentous event that had transpired in their small home.

Juan Pablo ran past the Rodriguezes' house and rushed behind the gas station again. If the cantina's grill was hot and Mario was cooking, the back door to the kitchen would be open. He hesitated before racing across the open space between the two buildings. Ignoring the familiar, once comforting scents rising from the cantina's kitchen, Juan Pablo stepped to the back door.

Breathing hard and fast, he looked in.

Mario's face was marred with fear as he tried to still the shaking in his hands before pouring the freshly made salsa into serving bowls. A large pot warmed the beans on the grill. The cantina's best steaks sizzled away. A pile of tortillas warmed there, too.

Juan Pablo stepped into the light.

Mario spotted him with a gasp.

Juan Pablo motioned for silence.

Mario cast a furtive glance at the men on the patio and looked back at the boy. He shook his head furiously, motioning for Juan Pablo to vamoose, to save himself, but instead the boy moved in swift, sure steps to the pot of beans. He unscrewed the lid to the jar and dumped all but an inch of the precious liquid into the pot. The rest was poured into the salsa. Mario's brows drew a sharp line across his wrinkled forehead. For a long moment, the old man stood staring stupidly at the boy.

Abruptly his face changed with the shock of what Juan Pablo was doing.

Juan Pablo nodded slowly.

Mario shoved him into the darkened pantry.

Terrified by what he had done, what was about to happen, Juan Pablo drew in the sweet scent of Mario's famous pan dulce, staring without seeing the bags of black beans, boxes of onions, bags of flour and corn, and cans lining the shelves. How long would the poison take? Five minutes? An hour? He didn't know.

Keeping to the shadows, Juan Pablo stepped out to watch.

Mario stirred the pot reverently now, as if the dark brown stew held their fates—and it did, it did. He hastily began preparing the plates. The men began shouting to hurry with the food. Mario had never moved faster.

It took four trips but finally all the men were served. Both groups of men gathered at two tables, side by side. Each man had a plate full of beans and a steak. The pan of tortillas sat alongside multiple bowls of salsa.

As the men ate greedily, ravenously, Mario returned to the kitchen to prepare pitchers of water along with another bottle of tequila and a bottle of rum as demanded. These too, soon sat on the table. Returning to the kitchen, he pretended to tend to pots and pans as he watched the food disappear amidst laughter and rancorous talk.

Inching further out of the pantry, mesmerized by the scene before him, Juan Pablo's heart fell in sync with the rhythmic thud of the music as he remembered that terrible day last year, the first hint that the long shadow of Mexico's problems had reached into Rosario.

That day he had come home to find Mario consulting with his abuela.

I can't go on Elena. At first it was one Federale, Fernando. A free dinner once in a while. Fine. The price of doing business, but Dios mío. Now he brings his amigos. I am supposed to feed sometimes ten men every other day. No tip, no nothing, barely a gracias. I cannot refuse. People have been killed or disappeared for less or they lose everything to a suspicious fire. I could not pay Leonardo's tuition this month—

Ah, his abuela had scoffed, her eyes smiling at her friend, *this trouble has a simple solution.*

The whole town knew the rest of the story. Two days later, the next time the federal officers showed up at the cantina, they ate and drank their fill before piling into their SUVs and driving off. That night Mario received a phone call from the hospital informing him that several of his customers had contracted food poisoning.

What did you give Mario, Abuela? he had asked in the days following.

Datura. It is a rare and beautiful flower, growing in marshes by rivers. The tiniest amount will make you wish for death.

You will die?

Not always, his abuela had said. *Sometimes you live if you are young and healthy and there is a hospital nearby.*

Now, as Juan Pablo watched and waited, he felt certain they would not actually die. He intended that they only wished they were dead, sick enough so they would not—could not—hurt Rocio. They were all young men, he told himself. They could probably get to the hospital in time.

He watched as the big man removed his phone. What was he doing? Taking a picture? No, a video. Holding it up, he swept the phone in a circular motion over the cantina's patio, stopping on a man sitting across from him. The man with the old woman's bun on top of his head.

Juan Pablo could not believe what happened next.

Carlos's gun appeared in his hand. "Hold still, amigo," he cautioned. All the men tensed, turning to Carlos as he took aim. The anxious moment collapsed as Carlos rubbed his hand down his face. "My vision is blurred. Geezus, this shit is potent." Blinking, undeterred, Carlos aimed and fired once.

The man's bun exploded.

The shock gave way to hearty laughter, continuing as the man reached to feel for his bun that was no longer there.

"Haircuts are free," Carlos joked, laughing at his comrade's terror. The men relaxed as their laughter died. Yet, his victim seemed frozen in time, his eyes bulging.

No one seemed to notice at first.

The noise continued over the booming beat of the music. They kept eating and drinking their fill. Finally, one by one, hands pushed plates aside. Pipes were passed around. Mario appeared with the pot of beans, but there were no takers. He tried not to look at the frozen man, a trickle of blood dripping over his thin lips.

"This shit is really tough," Carlos said, grabbing the sides of his head to stop the strange sensations burning through him. "Jesus, I am . . . high."

"Sí. I can't get a breath . . ."

"Water," Rencor demanded. "I need . . ."

He never finished as he was stopped by what seemed some great internal shock.

Mario rushed inside to fetch more water. He filled the pitcher and began gathering glasses onto a tray, but his hands shook badly. He pressed them against his thighs, took a deep breath, and offered up a prayer.

Juan Pablo came slowly out from hiding.

"Jesus. What's wrong with Kooch?"

Just like the first victim, the man Carlos referred to sat staring dumbly into space, his eyes unblinking and bulging hideously. His hands wrapped around his throat as if he was choking himself to death.

"Dios mío. I can't see," said another man furiously rubbing his eyes. The man Rencor grabbed the table. "Hilado . . . alto, alto . . ." Just like that he toppled out of his chair and onto the floor, convulsing violently.

The man next to him emitted a stream of vomit onto the floor.

Swear words and screams blasted forth in unison, louder even than the music.

"What the . . . ?" A man's last word stopped as his mouth began foaming. Bubbles of spit erupted over his lips just as he, too, started jerking as if electrocuted.

Chaos erupted all at once. Shouts and screams and cries for help.

Juan Pablo stepped forward to watch.

Within minutes five of the men writhed in agony on the floor, clutching their bellies as they convulsed in tight balls.

Sweat poured off Carlos's face and he suddenly lurched forward, ejecting a grotesque stream of puke over the table. He fell face-first into it, his body shaking violently.

Breathing in pained grunts, wiping the sweat from his eyes as he gripped the table, the giant bodyguard stood unsteadily to assist his boss, but stopped, seized by an internal agony. With a loud warlike cry, the big man fell backward, toppling like a tree and crashing onto a table. He moved no more.

Juan Pablo tensed for one moment as one of the last men alive managed to get his machine gun into his hands, but in the few seconds he tried to determine who he should shoot, the gun dropped and he fell over with uncontrollable shaking.

Only two men remained seated, but only one was still alive. The Peacock, with the damning trophies of his victims' hair, managed to stand on unsteady legs. He looked up from the dying men that surrounded him and suddenly found Juan Pablo. Their eyes locked, the key tossed away. "You . . ." he began with a soft viciousness, but he was breathing in huge, unnatural heaves. ". . . don't know what you've done . . . persona estúpida . . ." He drew his gun and he took one, then two steps.

Mario stepped in front of Juan Pablo just as the man dropped to his knees with a scream of gut-ripping pain. Then he, too, dropped first to his knees, the gun falling, and then he fell over.

Only three men still shook now, but their bodies no longer produced the violent shaking, only a small tremble of their muscles' last grip on life.

In minutes even these stopped.

Retrieving the last bottle of Tequila and a glass, Mario folded himself at the table furthest away. He started to pour a drink, but stopped, his disbelieving gaze staring at the scene from a horror movie.

The old man burst into silent tears of relief.

As if in a dream, without any real consciousness, Juan Pablo went to the box and turned the music off. The sudden silence was broken by a steady pounding sounding as if from far away. It came as a start to realize the loud thud was the cry of his own heart.

CHAPTER TWO

Juan Pablo raced up the stairs to Rocio.

Within minutes of the last awful death, he appeared in the doorway of the bedroom. Rocio was handcuffed to the bed. Her expression held his same shock, but desperation too, more scared than he could know.

"JP," Rocio cried, "what's happening? I heard the cries and screams, but—"

"I poured my abuela's bottle of datura into the beans."

The girl's dark eyes searched his face. "A whole bottle?"

Juan Pablo nodded. "I had to make sure all of them would be sick."

"Are they all . . . ?"

He nodded again. "I didn't mean to kill them, but I couldn't let them hurt you. I just couldn't."

Tears suddenly replaced the fear in Rocio's eyes.

"Are you okay, Rocio?"

"I was so afraid . . . I . . . ." The girl's lip trembled. "I kept thinking . . . I thought . . . ." She couldn't finish. "You saved me, JP."

Shaken to the core, he came to the edge of the bed. Rocio had only cried two other times: when her mother left for a job in America and last year when her own abuela had transitioned from life. It unnerved him now, triggering an understanding of the magnitude of what he had done.

He had killed eight men . . .

For several minutes he tried to remove the handcuffs, only to realize he wasn't thinking straight. He needed the key.

Rocio said, "The key. He put it in his pocket. The grande monster."

Juan Pablo nodded before rushing back down the stairs. He slowed as he approached the patio, half expecting at least one of them to recover enough to shoot him. He studied the scene for a long minute. He counted eight bodies, all but the one on the floor. There was no movement whatsoever now. An unnatural stillness mixed with the stench of vomit but he ignored this. He was thinking instead of the time he asked his abuela about hell.

Abuela, if you do not believe in hell, then what happens to bad people when they die? Do they become Sky People, too?

Sometimes, she had said.

That doesn't seem right.

Sky People are immersed in the energy of love, in a way we cannot imagine. It gives them a great wisdom and bad people view their deeds through a prism of a boundless compassion. You are too young to understand, but there can be no greater punishment for a soul.

This still didn't seem right, and he had pressed with another question. *What about the very worst people, people who kill and hurt many people; people who like to hurt other people?*

Some souls do not return to the sky.

What happens to them?

They cease to be.

He would like to believe this now.

Juan Pablo patted the pocket on the giant's trousers. He felt a phone. Feeling something in the other pocket, he lifted the side of it and slipped his hand in. He withdrew small plastic bags of powder. Some kind of drug. Tossing them aside, he abruptly noticed a key ring on his belt.

A phone rang to life.

Juan Pablo's gaze flew to Carlos, head still stuck in a puddle of vomit.

Washed in renewed panic, he waited through six rings.

Urged to speed by the sound, the nightmarish situation, he ripped the keys from the belt. Clasped in his hand, he stood just as the bodyguard's phone rang "La Cucaracha." It rang ten times before going silent. He started to move when Carlos's phone rang again.

Two more phones started ringing.

Mario stood up in alarm as another phone sounded and another. Amidst the cacophony of demanding phones, the old man shouted, his hand waving, "Vamoose, Juan Pablo, vamoose."

Juan Pablo rushed upstairs and burst into the bedroom. He fell upon Rocio with the keys. "Their phones."

"I hear them."

"They are all ringing."

"I don't understand," Rocio said. "What does it mean?"

"They'll be sending an army out to find out what happened. We've got to get out of here."

Once freed, they rushed downstairs.

Juan Pablo's arm shot out protectively. Rocio's hands flew to her mouth to stop a scream even as she stared at the scene drawn from a nightmare. Two phones still rang, but the others fell into a more ominous silence. Her eyes found her grandfather.

"I'll get my truck," Mario said.

"No, no," Juan Pablo said. "There is only one road out. They will be coming up it."

"You and Rocio can go out the Butterfly Pass through the sanctuary," Juan Pablo said.

Mario's gaze landed on the young man.

The residents and tourists all came and went on the main road. None of them had ever been on the famous twenty-three kilometer trail through the mountains and forest the other way. They knew of it only from the occasional hikers (hippy types, usually German or American) who arrived at the opposite end of town, the butterfly sanctuary, rather than the road leading to the plaza. Because of his excellent English, Juan Pablo met many of these hikers as they came to the meadow where he practiced his violin or as they passed by the front of his house. They were always covered in dirt, ragged, and starving but in a state of ecstasy brought by a million butterflies floating and gliding in the sky. These hikers were also the poorest people on earth. They often asked if he knew where they could trade work for something to eat. His abuela fixed them a hot meal: tortillas and beans, eggs, fried cornbread, and jam as he translated the stories of their journeys for his abuela's enjoyment.

The Butterfly Pass was the only way to escape the fury of wrath and vengeance heading toward them.

"Rocio, get your things," Mario ordered. "Only what you can carry. Save room for water and food."

Rocio nodded and flew upstairs again.

"You too, Juan Pablo. Hurry."

Juan Pablo turned back to his house, his thoughts flying even faster than his feet. He could not leave his abuela. With neither a mother nor a father, she was the only thing separating him from being an orphan; he would be lost without her. He would never leave her alone to the uncertain mercy of these droguistas. Just as he had protected Rocio, he would find a means to keep his abuela safe.

Opening the door to his house, he found the old woman, still unconscious on the small cot, the blanket tucked under her chin. He moved to the lamp and turned it on. Light flooded the space and he greeted the second miracle.

Like the final signature to a beautiful painting, the giant monarch had taken its last flight and settled on his abuela's forehead. It was impossible, of course, but there it was.

Both butterfly and old woman moved no more.

The magical sight blurred.

Juan Pablo dropped to his knees. He took the still-warm, weathered old hand in his for the last time and brought it to his lips to kiss.

"Te amo, Abuela. Te amo . . ."

CHAPTER THREE

Rocio and Mario found him kneeling over Elena, silent tears falling over the old lady's still and lifeless form. Mario dropped to his knees and gave the sign of the cross, while Rocio came quietly behind Juan Pablo and put her arms around him. Closing her eyes, she rested her head on his back.

The warm embrace told him he was not alone in his grief.

They never knew how long they knelt there, crying over the old woman they all loved, five minutes, maybe more, but Mario abruptly interrupted the quiet and said the strangest thing, "I hear her. I hear Elena . . ."

Blinking furiously, Juan Pablo looked at Mario for the explanation of these words.

"Abuelo?" Rocio whispered.

"¡Ándale! she says. She must be buried in the butterflies, she says. ¡Ándale! ¡Ándale!"

Rocio's eyes widened. "Because they are coming." She understood this at once. "It is the only chance. Of course, Elena must be buried with the butterflies."

The girl's urging managed to penetrate Juan Pablo's thick curtain of grief. "¡Ándale! ¡Ándale!" She repeated as she stood up. "We must bury Elena before they get here!"

Juan Pablo nodded, wiping at his face. His abuela had always insisted she be buried in the butterflies.

Juan Pablo, when I transition to the Sky People, I want my body buried in the butterflies.

Please, Abuela, do not transition for a long, long time, he had replied. The very idea of her leaving him alone seemed terrifying.

On unsteady feet, Juan Pablo rose. Using the blanket, Rocio and Mario had already lifted her body into the air. He started to grab the opposite end of the blanket that Rocio held.

Again, Mario froze and looked this way and that. "She is saying violin, violin!"

Juan Pablo swallowed, nodding as if he had heard this too.

His most prized possession. More than a possession, it was a part of him. When he was just five, his abuela had given him the precious family heirloom, the violin that had belonged to his beautiful mother and her father before her. It was not just any violin, but a Charles Bailly violin, made in France over a hundred years ago. Señor Tapis, a once famous musician, had mysteriously arrived in El Rosario shortly after this—a feat no doubt arranged by his abuela. He had given him lessons every day until his passing two years ago.

He had taken to the instrument like one of their butterflies to the sky. Both his teacher and his abuela believed his soul held music in the same way a pupa holds a butterfly; like his mother, and her father before that, he had been born with it, the music had just waited to manifest.

Juan Pablo rushed to this treasure and threw it over his shoulder before he found his backpack and quickly secured all the seeds in the house as well as the almond milk. He rushed back and took his place at the other end of the blanket. In this way, the three of them began the long journey into their last night in El Rosario.

The urgency of their mission, to bury the old lady before the banditos arrived, renewed their fear and for a brief spell, it overwhelmed their sadness and grief.

Rocio turned on her phone's flashlight and held it in her mouth. Juan Pablo and Rocio clutched the edge of the blanket at his abuela's head and Mario grasped the blanket at her feet. They would bury Elena in the butterfly meadow at the top of the sanctuary. Of all the people who ever lived, of course Elena must be buried beneath the loose soil made of an echelon of billions of butterflies. They owed the old woman this final wish.

Time pressed on them. Burdened with heavy packs full of everything too dear to leave behind, they made slow progress up the mountain. They had only minutes before the narco-traffickers showed up, discovered their dead comrades, and turned their attention to finding the culprits.

Rocio stumbled and with a whoosh, fell backside to the ground. The corner of the blanket jerked from Juan Pablo's hands, and weighed down by his violin case and backpack full of almond milk, he lost his footing and slid. Gravel cut into his bare hands. Elena's lifeless body and the two shovels crashed into Rocio, but the girl caught her scream in a gasp.

They held still for a long moment on the cold ground, assessing the situation.

Finding her phone first, Rocio swept the dim light in a wide arch to the sky.

"Easy, easy," Mario whispered, his own breath ragged and strained. The old man set down his end of the blanket on the darkened landscape and stood up to massage the pain shooting down his arm and through his back. The hoot of an owl interrupted the unnatural quiet of the forest. The distant sound barely registered over their frightened breaths, especially Mario's. It took several tense moments to set things right again and continue on.

Giant fir trees, the famous oyamel forest of the butterflies, crowded the worn hiking trail on all sides. Rocks, some the size of a foot, treacherously littered their way, but Rocio's careful orchestration of the phone's light allowed them to sidestep the worse pivots. Just when Juan Pablo's arms began to shake with the exertion, the trees at last gave way to the familiar open space of his and Rocio's meadow, the main stage of their childhood.

"Aquí estamos," Mario managed between irregular gasps.

They set their burden down and breathing hard and fast, they assessed the surroundings.

"The middle." Rocio's nod indicated the direction.

Picturing the meadow in the bright light of a full moon, Juan Pablo knew his abuela would approve of this final resting place. It was after all, her favorite place, where she often communed with the returning butterflies.

What do the butterflies tell you?

Oh, many things. They tell me of their journey across the great distance; of strong winds, friendly rains, and deadly ones; they sing, always, of their glorious sun. In these last years, they tell of the changes, too.

What changes?

The wind mostly, but also disappearing water and forests and milkweed plants. Fires, too, sometimes. More and more of them are returning to the Sky People . . .

"Come. ¡Ándale!" Mario said, struggling out of his backpack. His breaths rose and fell with an unusual strain. They were all perspiring and bone tired, and after the fear they had just lived through, continued to live through, it was little wonder the old man could not quite catch his breath. For a long moment, he bent over his knees, just trying to ease the pain in his chest. "Rocio, stand back there and watch for any sign . . . of people."

Rocio nodded before turning her anxious gaze to the dark trail behind them.

In the far distance down the mountain, El Rosario appeared as a patch of pitch-blackness. There were no lights now. They had demolished all lights at the cantina as soon as they gathered their things and began the journey up the mountain.

They took turns digging the loose soil made of centuries of butterflies. The grave had to be deep enough to prevent any unearthing by coyotes, but after that, no one figured it ultimately mattered how deep she was buried.

"¡Ándale!" Mario kept whispering.

Juan Pablo didn't think, he only moved, swinging the shovel into the dirt and lifting it out. Had he entertained a thought, he would drop to his knees and cry for all that had happened, all that was happening. His abuela had died and he was burying her in the meadow of butterflies and music. He was an orphan, a creature he had always, his whole life, pitied, but found in his pity an extreme gratitude for his abuela's love. He had just murdered eight men; he had watched the life leave their bodies. He was running away from the only home he had ever known, a place he only now realized how much he loved.

"Okay, okay," Mario said. "Help me lift our dear old lady one last time."

They placed her body into the shallow grave.

Mario and Juan Pablo began covering the grave with the small piles of dirt surrounding it, his abuela's body mixed forever with a millennium of butterflies.

He would not cry more now.

Nor could he speak. No words could express the depth of his loss. Not now. Not ever.

Rocio came and took Juan Pablo's hand in hers, and her abuelo offered a simple eulogy: "We love you, Elena." Mario paused, wiping his brow with his sleeve, still trying to ease his ragged breathing. "The whole town has always loved you, a soul full of the Holy Spirit and as beautiful as the butterflies that sustain us." He coughed, and required several anxious minutes to recover. "You are the best person I've ever known. I promise I will take care of Juan—"

The old man suddenly drew a sharp breath, but the inhale stopped. Juan Pablo forgot to breathe, waiting for Mario's.

The shovel dropped from the old man's hands. Mario's next inhale came as a loud, gurgling wheeze.

Rocio called out as she hit his back. "Abuelo, Abuelo!"

Juan Pablo watched in sick horror as Mario's hands clutched at his chest and he dropped to the ground. Rocio fell over him, gently shaking him, calling his name.

Rocio collapsed over his body.

Juan Pablo's startled senses snapped back in an instant. He lifted Rocio up and using all his strength he turned the body over.

Rocio covered her trembling mouth, even as she whispered "abuelo" over and over, trying to call him back to this life. Juan Pablo called to the stricken man too, before he placed his hand over the old man's chest. In desperation, he pounded Mario's chest in the way he had seen it done in movies, but after several minutes, he gave up the fierce, but futile, movement. He put his head against the old man's chest, but felt no heart beating there. He leaned over and put his cheek on Mario's lips to feel for a breath.

Juan Pablo stumbled to his feet, shocked more than anything, and acting on instinct, he reached for Rocio.

The girl clung to him as if her life depended on it.

Juan Pablo closed his eyes. "I'm so sorry, Rocio. I'm so sorry . . ."

Juan Pablo had lost his abuela and Rocio had lost her abuelo, but it was even more than that. They had both lost the person who had always cared for them. They had lost the only home either of them had ever known. They were in danger of losing even more. They were in danger of losing their lives.

They could not afford the luxury of grief now.

"Rocio, Rocio, we have to keep going."

But Rocio dropped to her knees and pressed her tear-stained face against her grandfather's body. "No, no," she whispered. "This cannot be . . ."

Kneeling down, he pulled Rocio forcibly up. "Rocio, Rocio, they're coming for us. We have to keep going."

She nodded, trying to slow her gasps and wipe her eyes.

A new and strange sound rose in the far distance.

Helicopters. Three of them circled the cantina far down the mountain. The bright floodlights lit the patio before stopping on the collection of bodies there.

A tense minute passed, maybe more before all three helicopters zoomed away, lights searching the town. One helicopter light slowly moved up the long row of houses on one side, while another went up the row on the left. The third helicopter rushed toward them. The headlights of three cars raced up the road leading to the plaza in the far distance.

"Grab your bags," Juan Pablo shouted.

Crying still, gulping in gasps of breath, Rocio turned to where their backpacks sat in a small pile. Juan Pablo rushed to his violin and backpack, heaving them onto his back. "The tepee."

Rocio grabbed her backpack. The two stared at Mario's pack.

"I'll get it," Juan Pablo said.

Nodding, Rocio turned on the flashlight on her phone to light the way.

"No, no, they will see it," Juan Pablo warned. With effort, he lifted Mario's heavy pack. Rocio aimed her phone to the ground and with trembling fingers she turned it off before looking down the mountain to where the helicopters circled. Stumbling with the weight of the pack Juan Pablo rushed behind Rocio into the overhead protection of the forest.

The sliver of moon lit the space around them. Earth crunched beneath their sneakers. The tepee lay hidden in a wide arch of brush, the entrance a small dark triangle. The black-and-white blankets that covered the wood structure were layered with sticks and brush. It was impossible to see from the outside, wasn't it?

At least it would be completely hidden from above.

Juan Pablo followed Rocio's hurried steps. Dropping to her knees, she disappeared through the entrance. Juan Pablo followed, emerging into pitch blackness. Rocio fumbled with her phone's light, safe inside the space, no bigger than the inside of a small car. Orange blankets covered the ground. On top, there was a bottle of water and two sodas alongside a stack of books—that was all.

Juan Pablo dropped the bags inside before turning to the entrance.

"Where are you going?" Rocio asked in a panic.

"I'll be right back."

A helicopter spotted the trailhead and headed up, the light flooding the area just below. Juan Pablo assessed the risk, but knew he had to do it. Nimble and quick without the weight of the packs, he flew back to the fallen Mario and fell beside his body. Using all his strength, he managed to turn him on his side, finding the gun behind his back, tucked into his belt. Pointing it at the ground and holding it carefully, he ran back to the safety of the tepee.

The helicopter noise drowned out everything, even his frantic thoughts.

Juan Pablo reached the edge of the trees and ducked behind a giant fir tree just as the helicopter zoomed into the meadow. Pressed backside against the trunk, he watched as the helicopter's light circled the open space and then stopped, hovering over Mario's dead body.

For a full three minutes, the helicopter hovered there, the pilot trying to make sense of it. Finally, it arced back into the blackened sky and returned to the trail. Juan Pablo used this time to make his way back to the tepee. He ducked inside.

"One helicopter is following the trail," he whispered. "The other two are still circling the town."

Wiping her eyes to stop crying, Rocio tried to see him in the darkness. "What will we do?"

Juan Pablo knew the answer. "We wait until they're gone, and then we make our way down the trail."

"But . . . if they find Abuelo's body?"

"They already have. The helicopter spotted it from above."

"They will investigate."

"But they will only find him. They might think he acted alone. They might search the area, but they will never find us in here." He said it with certainty, though he wasn't at all sure that the tepee would be missed. No one had ever found them here, but then no one had ever searched for them before.

They fell into silence, interrupted only by the soft sound of Rocio's tears. "Elena and now Abuelo . . ." The noise of the first helicopter drifted further away even as the other two drew progressively nearer. He and Rocio pulled closer to each other.

The noise increased dramatically when Juan Pablo would have sworn this was not possible. He guessed the two helicopters now hovered over the meadow, as the pilots studied the dead body, communicating both with each other and with the men on the ground, no doubt. The joint sound split suddenly and the tremendous roar of the helicopters circling the area rose and fell. They were looking for more people.

The men at the plaza would be examining the dead bodies there. It would not take Einstein to figure out they had been poisoned.

They would no doubt be searching the houses, but they were all empty now. They would find nothing. Even if they did discover the poison had come from his abuela's house, what could they do? No one was there now. No one lived there anymore.

He had no home. No parents. Rocio had no home. Her mother and brother were in faraway countries. They faced a gang of criminals and murderers alone. It was up to him to keep Rocio safe.

A helicopter's searchlight swung back and forth above. He pulled Rocio even closer. They looked up, as if they could see the light arcing above them. After a moment or two, it drew away and returned to the meadow.

Juan Pablo drew a deep breath of relief.

The first helicopter returned. Now, the three helicopters hung over the meadow, drowning out all other sounds.

If only he could see what they were doing.

Abruptly, Juan Pablo realized there were men on the ground in the meadow.

Juan Pablo had no idea how long they waited, crouched in the tepee, bound by fear and apprehension, crying softly and blurting a "I cannot believe this is happening . . ." until it was a habit, these words. At some point the helicopters took off, one by one. The men in the meadow retreated as well.

Gradually they became aware of the stillness, shot straight from heaven, a balm to their frayed nerves.

"I think they're gone," Rocio whispered.

Juan Pablo nodded. "Sí," he said, "for now. Can you sleep?"

Poised on the edge of hysteria, Rocio let out a pained yelp.

"I am going to see if I can tell what is happening," Juan Pablo said.

"No." Desperation filled Rocio's whisper. "No. Stay here, JP."

"I'll just be a minute," he whispered back. "I'll be careful."

Holding the gun awkwardly, having no idea how to shoot it, Juan Pablo slipped outside into the dark forest. He held still, listening for any sound and letting his eyes adjust to the moonlit darkness. Not even the owl hooted now. He quietly made his way back to the edge of the trees and peered out into the darker space of the meadow.

There was no one and nothing. They had even taken Mario's body.

Like a warning, the mistake rang loud in Juan Pablo's mind. The shovels. They had left both shovels. They would know someone had helped Mario bury the old woman.

They'd be looking for another person.

He cautiously made his way to where they had buried his abuela. Sure enough, the shovels were gone.

Down the mountain, he saw that all activity had returned to the town. At least a dozen headlights went both ways on the road leading into and out of El Rosario. The lanterns at the cantina were turned on again, now bright against the darkness. Two houses were lit as well. They had begun a house-to-house search.

The Gonzalezes' house light came on as he watched. It was two doors down from his abuela's house. They would soon be inside his house with all of his abuela's jars of potions and herbs. They would know the poison had come from there, but no one remained. Would the information mean anything?

Juan Pablo found his way back to the safety of the tepee.

"JP," Rocio said, relief plain in her tone, "what's happening?"

"They are searching the houses one by one. There are a dozen cars now. They are probably removing the bodies. I think we are safe for now," he lied, wishing he believed it. "I will stay awake while you sleep."

"I can't sleep. I'll never be able to sleep again."

Juan Pablo put his arm around her and she leaned against him.

They sat in a frightened silence for a long time. Juan Pablo's thoughts kept turning in circles around the idea of escaping. He must do everything possible to keep Rocio from being caught, even if it meant sacrificing his own life. He alone had a chance of surviving an interrogation . . .

A plan emerged in his mind's eye. If at any time it seemed they might discover their hideout, he would slip away and make his way down the hill. Once near the town, he would fire the gun. This would draw their attention to the area and away from Rocio. Hopefully, he could escape into the forest and evade capture. If they did catch him, he would say he knew nothing of the poison and had been hiding the whole time, that Mario had told him to hide in the forest. Hopefully, they would not kill him, and Rocio would gain enough time to escape.

If they could make their way down the Butterfly Pass, he and Rocio knew how to get to Guadalajara. A bus could take them to Puerto Vallarta, and another could bring them down to her uncle's fishing village. They could do it. They would make it.

If they escaped undetected from the mountain.

CHAPTER FOUR

Juan Pablo did not remember falling asleep. Like Rocio, he would not have thought it possible, but at some point he must have. Because the next thing he knew, morning light flooded from above and he opened his eyes. Rocio lay next to him, sound asleep, one arm crooked and thrown back, her tasseled hair forming a dark halo around her head.

Muffled sounds of men talking in the meadow reached him.

He held still, listening.

He couldn't make out what they were saying or even how many there were. He heard the words *reward . . . got . . . somewhere . . . couldn't . . . far.* Other voices joined them before disappearing, swallowed by distance and the trees between them.

He thought they were gone, but no. Boots crunched over the forest floor nearby.

"Here . . . and here," a man said. "Footsteps, no?"

"Look. Dozens of footsteps all over. It's a goddamn tourist spot, sí?"

"He's got to be somewhere. He couldn't have gone far."

They sounded twenty meters away. Juan Pablo held his breath.

"We will find him."

"If we don't, the Hunter will."

"Axel says he's on his way. The boss offered him half a million for the kill. He wants him that bad."

"You think he's one of the Vetas?"

"Knives and bullets, sí, but poison? It is not their way. This was that old man, acting with a partner. The old woman probably got a

49

taste. Maybe accidental, maybe not. They probably smoked her to stop her from singing."

Reliving the horrors of the night, Rocio made a faint cry in her sleep.

The tiny whisper of a noise played like the crash of symbols in Juan Pablo's mind and he froze, his heart leaping as if running.

"All these butterflies, ¡Dios mío!"

"My mother made a paste out of butterflies . . . for tortillas. Good if you are very hungry."

The boots stomped back toward the meadow.

He sat in tense stillness and minutes piled onto minutes. Maybe an hour passed, but at some point he realized there were no more voices. All was quiet against the backdrop of the soft sounds of Rocio's slumber.

He had to pee. He had to risk it.

Cautiously, he rose from the tepee. He took a dozen steps and relieved himself in the bushes. He stole a quick glance in the direction of the meadow. No one and nothing moved, but he could not see through the trees.

Butterflies drifted in the morning sunlight, lighting on branches and soaking up the new sun, either late arriving or reluctant to leave—no one, not even his abuela, could ever say with certainty. Roosting doves cooed nearby. A couple of sparrows flew this way and that, avoiding the butterflies. (Milkweed made the butterflies taste horrible, so very few birds ate them.) A rabbit sat munching on the edge of the meadow, unmindful of the calamity that had just occurred.

Juan Pablo watched the small creature come suddenly upright. He heard the Humvee's engine before he saw it. He ducked behind a tree just as it roared into the meadow. He pressed himself against the trunk.

He shouldn't have left the safety of the tepee.

Men jumped out of the black Humvee.

"Okay. We need to find the bastard before the Hunter."

"No matter what it takes. You four follow the trail at least fifteen kilometers. Keep your eyes open. He's in there somewhere. The birds will be flying all day."

The chorus of "yes, boss" sounded like the grunts of livestock.

"We'll drive back around and head up from the other end. If we don't find him today, we should meet halfway somewhere before midnight and we will set up camp. Then reverse our course in the morning. We've got a roadblock at the other end, so he is trapped. Let's go."

Four men set off on the trail. Juan Pablo inched his way behind the tree as they marched forward. The other men returned to the Humvee. The giant vehicle started and turned back to town.

Juan Pablo waited until he heard no sound in either direction before he quietly, stealthily made his way back to the tepee. He slipped inside, only to find Rocio upright, staring in terror, as if he was the banditos.

Rocio fell on him with a hug. "When you weren't here, I was— oh, JP."

Rocio's greeting took him aback. She was trembling with fear.

He told her what he had heard.

"How long will they be searching for us?"

"Days, it sounds like," Juan Pablo said. "He said the helicopters, birds, they call them, were coming back, too."

Rocio grew more anxious still. "We will have to stay hidden like this . . . for—"

"Two days maybe," Juan Pablo finished for her. "But Rocio, Rocio," he said her name twice for emphasis, "it will be all right. When they give up searching for us, we can make our way out. Sí, they have a roadblock at the end of the trail, and if it is still there when we reach it, we will have to find a way around it. But then we can hitch a ride to Guadalajara and take a bus from there."

Rocio turned the plan over in her mind.

Juan Pablo didn't mention this mystery Hunter. He was scared enough for both of them.

They discussed the danger for over an hour before Rocio confessed she had to pee. Juan Pablo slipped outside to make sure it was safe. No one moved in the meadow. He gave a brief whistle, signaling that it was clear before standing guard while she hurriedly relieved herself.

Once back in the tepee, Rocio began organizing the packs so they would be ready to leave as soon as it was safe. They had eight bottles of almond milk. Elena believed almond milk was much healthier to drink than regular milk, not to mention cheaper, and both she and Mario kept a huge supply on hand. Juan Pablo had the smart idea that since almond milk and water weighed the same, they should fill the water bottles with the almond milk.

He shot a prayer of thanks for this gift now.

Additionally, Rocio had packed a large jar of peanut butter, a stack of tortillas, a loaf of bread, and two apples. Juan Pablo found a box of cereal, two carefully wrapped hard-boiled eggs, and three bananas in Mario's pack. Because his abuela had been ill for a week, Juan Pablo had not found much to bring, even if he had been able to think straight in the aftermath of finding his abuela gone. Besides the milkweed seeds, he only had a canister of hemp seeds his abuela always sprinkled on his food for added nutrition.

Stomachs rumbling, Rocio used Juan Pablo's knife to spread peanut butter and hemp seeds on a tortilla for each of them. They each ate an egg. They split one of the sodas they'd been saving in the tepee for a special occasion.

Once full, they lay down as best they could in the small space.

The long wait began.

If they could somehow take away the fear, it might have been like any other free afternoon. He and Rocio lay side by side in mutual silence. Any sound might alert a bandito to their presence.

Thoughts of his abuela crept into this quiet.

The idea that the old woman no longer walked the earth seemed impossible. How he loved her and she him, showering him with enough love to make up for a missing mother and father. Whenever they parted, she pulled him close and reached up to kiss his forehead. To his abuela, hugs were a miracle medicine that all people needed and no one got enough of and she happily dispensed this remedy to everyone.

He sometimes thought she knew as much as Google. She often made him read his science textbooks or the science section of the newspaper out loud, feeling enormous pride when a scientist or group of researchers discovered something she already knew.

It seems odd, Abuela, how much you love science.

The old woman chopped vegetables from the garden for dinner. *I do indeed. What a great mountain of knowledge scientists collect! Have you ever noticed, Juan Pablo, how this mountain of knowledge keeps growing? One unlocked mystery leads to ten more mysteries in the cosmic geometry of infinity.*

Stories, too, she loved to listen to stories. Almost every night of his life, when he finally tucked his violin away, he and Abuela and sometimes Rocio, too, read together. At first, when he was younger, she was testing his reading ability in English, but later, it was just to enjoy a good book.

Images of his abuela played through his mind's eye: the old woman tossing her head back and laughing, not a small sound either, but a big, booming noise that defied her elf-like size; the wrinkled face beaming with pleasure at the conclusion to any difficult piece he played well; the comically prideful look that appeared whenever she cured a person.

I am amazed you understand what they are teaching at your age, she said once after watching him listen to a Khan Academy math tutorial.

It is not even hard, this one. The professor makes it very simple.

You are very lucky, Juan Pablo. Being smart is the second greatest gift.

What is the first?

Kindness.

And she was kind. Their neighbors and children and the multitudes of tourists: rich and poor, young and old, happy or cross, his abuela always answered people with a warm smile and a good word. Time and again, he watched comments from his abuela, even just one, lift people up. Even strangers warmed to his abuela, and always seemed to reach out to touch her, as if for luck.

Abuela, why do people always touch you?

I am very close to the Sky People.

Most of all, he loved how much his abuela loved him.

Rocio must have noticed his tears, because she slipped her hand in his.

"She will always be with us. We will be carrying her with us all our lives."

Nodding, he squeezed her hand. It sometimes seemed as if they owed everything that was good inside to her large and special presence in their lives. Their love of music and books, animals and forests. Even this, that he and Rocio spoke in English, owed itself to his abuela. From his birth, the old woman insisted he know English and Spanish both. She had convinced Rocio's mom of the same. Much of his abuela's medical education had been in English and she was very fluent. She insisted her grandson's English would be perfect; he would not just be fluent, but as comfortable in English as Spanish. Why she insisted was a mystery; she claimed only that *language was nourishment for the human brain, like water to a thirsty flower*—and the more the better.

Mornings until twelve were the English hours, the rest Spanish time. Yet, as they grew up, feeling special, Rocio and he only spoke English together. They could trade secrets with impunity. They watched almost all movies in English. They Googled only English, but they read books in both.

"I didn't tell you what Abuela said. Her last words to me."

"What?"

He told her the strange tale of their last conversation.

Rocio lifted up on her elbow. "America. She wants you to go to America?"

"Sí. She said to follow the butterfly path to Baja to Tijuana and into California. She said I must reach Pacific Grove by summer's end. The last thing she said was that he will be waiting for me there."

Rocio's eyebrows drew together. "Who will be waiting for you?"

"I don't know."

"Your father?"

For reasons he did not know, his abuela did not like talking about his father.

I know all about my mother and her music, and I know she died giving birth to me, but what about my father, Abuela? What was his name?

Dr. Juan Laves.

My mother named me after him? He was a doctor?

Not a medical doctor, but the other kind. A scientist. She met him right here, when he came to Rosario to study the butterflies and she was visiting.

Maybe he is still alive. Maybe we can find him, Abuela? Maybe he has a Facebook page.

Strange emotions crossed his abuela's face. *Go ahead. Try if you want to.*

He tried off and on for years, but there was no trace of any doctor by that name. He even searched obituaries online, even though his abuela said that American hospitals never let people die, even when their spirit has transitioned to the sky. The American hospitals often kept dead bodies hooked up to machines that breathed for them and kept an illusion of life. People paid companies that paid the hospitals to maintain the illusion. Americans, she felt, were a very clever people, but often wasteful of their riches.

It was as if his father never really existed.

Are you sure my father is Juan Laves?

That was his name.

Only later did he realize how very unlikely this was—that his father was a Mexican-American butterfly scientist. His abuela must have made it up. Maybe she didn't know his real father or maybe she hadn't approved of him. He didn't know.

What was he like, Abuela? All I know about him was that he was a scientist who studied butterflies.

Your father was cheerful, very tall, and smart, like you.

How do you know he was smart?

There were many letters surrounding his name.

Abuela, be serious. How did you know he was smart?

He loved your mother's music as much as he loved your mother.

What else do you remember about my father?

What else, what else, she repeated. *He liked to sing to the butterflies.*

Sing to the butterflies? Like I play my violin to them?

No, not like that. He sang to the butterflies because they were the only creatures that didn't mind hearing the sounds his voice made.

He laughed then. *Abuela, you are teasing me. Sometimes I cannot tell what is real and what you imagine is real.*

Perhaps it doesn't matter. What is reality but a collection of beliefs, one after another, piled on top of each other, like sentences in a book. When you turn the last page, you realize very few were true, but somehow the whole created a picture of life.

Unfortunately, his abuela sometimes made no sense like that.

"I think she made up my father. Probably because the reality is too painful."

"To tell you the truth," Rocio confessed, "my mom and Abuelo always suspected this. They, too, thought the story of the butterfly scientist was—"

Juan Pablo motioned for silence as he abruptly sat up.

"Is it the helicopters again?" Rocio asked.

Juan Pablo shook his head. "Worse. It's a dog."

The distant sound of a dog barking drew closer.

"A search dog?" Rocio asked. They were fans of Animal Planet shows and they had once seen a show on search dogs. It showed how certain dogs could trace a scent over miles and miles, finding missing people, outlaws, or in a disaster, dead people.

Maybe the Hunter used a dog to search out his prey.

"If it is, we're in trouble."

Fear returned to Rocio's face in an instant.

"I'll lead them away," Juan Pablo said.

"No, no," Rocio protested. "You could get hurt. And if they find you—"

"I will just tell them I don't know anything. I'm just a teenager. I'll say Mario did it. Probably they won't kill me. But you, Rocio." Their eyes met and the horrible knowledge was acknowledged. "Different story."

He would not think. He would just do what he had to do.

Determined, he slipped outside of the tepee into the warm spring morning. He tucked the revolver in his Levi's and took off running.

He made out the sound of a dog, men shouting behind it.

He sprinted along the edge of the meadow, heading down the mountain. Going faster now, he ran until he reached the forest on the other side, away from the tepee. He stopped, breathing faster now, waiting a moment to catch sight of the dog. The dog needed to pick up his scent, and not Rocio in the tepee.

A crow squawked above, lifting into the air. Two sparrows joined the black bird just as a German shepherd–type dog burst into the meadow. The dog picked up a scent and circled the meadow nose to ground. Round and round he went in ever-tighter circles. The dog quickly came to his abuela's grave where he stood alert and sniffing. He suddenly looked up, straight at him.

The dog leapt into a run. The chase was on.

Juan Pablo ran down the forested hill. Dried leaves and branches crunched underfoot. He half slid, half stumbled. The barking was so close. Thinking the dog would tear him to bits, he looked up into the trees for a branch to climb. There was nothing he could reach. Breathing hard and fast, he raced down the hill. The dog sounded closer and closer still.

Juan Pablo stopped and turned around.

He ignored the drone of a beehive above. No time to spot it now.

Paws to the ground, the dog stopped too, barking like crazy, staring, looking as if he was about to pounce. But he didn't. He just stood there barking at him.

In a moment's inspiration, he remembered once a Middle Eastern tourist had stood at the plaza, terrified by little Tajo. Tajo's hair lifted and he barked uncertainly.

Look at Tajo, Juan Pablo, his abuela noticed.

He's scared of that lady?

Mario called Tajo back to the patio. Tail tucked between his legs, the little guy kept looking back as he came to Mario.

Dogs smell emotions the way we see emotions on faces.

Emotions? This information surprised him.

Sí. Tajo was confused by the lady's fear. Why is the lady afraid of me, Tajo wonders. (His abuela was always giving voice to the animals, saying what they were thinking.) *The fear scares them; they imagine they will be attacked by this terrified person and they can either run away or fight. People who are afraid of dogs always get bit by them.* She released a sigh. *Americans have a clever phrase for it:* vicious cycle.

Swallowing his fear as best he could, Juan Pablo knelt down and reached out his hand. "Hey, puppy," he said in a high, sing-song voice. "Easy there . . . easy."

The dog stopped barking and stared in confusion. He cocked his head, as if to say, "What are you up to there?" He hesitantly wagged his tail.

People think dogs wag their tails to show they are happy, but dogs wag their tail to throw their scent into the air, so you can smell their emotion.

But we don't smell emotions.

Ah, dogs do not know this.

The dog whimpered, then barked, but a different kind of bark. The creature looked around to the meadow, then back to Juan Pablo. He lowered to all fours, still as if he might spring back into action.

"It's okay, puppy," Juan Pablo continued in this manner.

The dog whimpered, his ears stuck straight up, alert with this unexpected situation. He backed up with uncertainty.

As his back paw came down, he suddenly yelped and his foot sprang high in the air. He tried to turn around to bite it. Yelping piteously, the injured leg lifted and lowered. The poor creature yelped every time the paw touched ground.

"What's wrong? What happened?"

He realized in an instant. The dog had stepped on a bee and it stung him.

Yet the dog stared at him with mistrust now, as if Juan Pablo had orchestrated his misfortune.

"Here. I'll help you," Juan Pablo started toward him.

Obviously frightened, the dog backed up as the boy stepped forward. He turned and hobbling on his injured paw, he kind of hopped away, looking back as if Juan Pablo might chase him now.

Juan Pablo could scarcely believe this bit of luck.

Wasting no time, he looked around for someplace to hide. Bramble bushes formed a tent between a group of three close trees. He made his way over and hurriedly parted the branches as best he could. Ducking down, he curled up and pulled the dead leaves and branches around him.

The men reached the meadow.

He heard their shouting, but couldn't make out the words.

A helicopter sounded in the distance, approaching fast.

The roar of the helicopter reached deafening levels and he covered his sensitive ears, trying to block it out. Crouched and tense, hiding like a frightened rabbit, he began to wonder if these men would ever give up. What if they didn't make it off the mountain? What if Rocio got caught by these people again?

His thoughts began turning in worried circles over the possibilities.

You look worried, Juan Pablo.

What's going to happen? I mean, what if—

What if, what if. The old woman dismissed this with a chuckle as she lifted a root-bound plant and set it in a bigger pot. *This what if is a made-up reality. Instead of choosing something that is distressing, choose something that lifts your spirits; choose something that makes you happy. Choose something fantastic.*

What if he and Rocio did manage to escape and make it to America?

The very thought made Juan Pablo's breath catch.

He imagined being a student in a music academy, a good one, surrounded by teachers and other students who shared his driving passion. He imagined playing in concerts before an audience. The joy of it quickened his heart, even as he sat still, crouched and scared like a hare. And what if Rocio got to go to an American school, a good one, where she got perfect marks and graduated with honors?

Happiness burst unexpectedly upon him.

A butterfly floated just beyond his hiding place.

He watched the delicate flight. Suspended between earth and sky. Was it late arriving? Or reluctant to leave?

He remembered the first time he found one of the infamous marked butterflies. He and his abuela had been hiking for kilometers, searching the forest floor for a rare mushroom at the end of summer. They might have missed it, but it appeared right at eye level.

Abuela, look. A white speck on its wing.

After studying this curiosity, her experienced fingers gently pinched the creature just so and lifted the white dot before setting the butterfly back in place. The discovery connected them to the Monarch Project. Thousands of people across North American found and caught butterflies, marking them with a tiny white speck that held a number. When someone found one of the marked butterflies, they took the number off and sent the information to the data center. In this way, the scientists had finally grasped the spectacular reach of the monarch butterflies' migration.

The project also revealed the steady decline of the creatures' once great numbers. The more he read about their butterflies, the more alarmed he became.

What if the butterflies do go extinct? What will happen to us? To all of us?

His abuela had set down her book. For a long moment she held perfectly still. In a whisper, he heard her speak in what-ifs, but like a prayer. *What if the world awakens to the danger we are facing here? What if the great World Wide Web unites all souls to the fate of the butterflies? What if this energy becomes a powerful force directed to saving them? What if, Juan Pablo, it is true, what the Sky People are telling me, that by saving the butterflies, we will be saving ourselves?*

The butterfly floated away and Juan Pablo hoped it was true, his abuela's what-if prayer. He tried to shift his cramped legs. He wanted to make a run for the tepee, but was it safe?

From the distance he heard the helicopter return, flying over first the meadow and then the town, disappearing. The hushed quiet of the forest returned. No human sounds came from the meadow.

Was it safe now?

Almost as if the question produced it, a butterfly flew directly in front of his hiding place. Juan Pablo watched it circle once, twice, then three times.

Why is three a magical number? he asked his abuela, for she seemed to always wait for threes.

Three reasons: the sun, the moon, and the earth; the trinity; the three sides of a triangle.

He knew this game. *Why not four?* he wondered, supplying, *"Water, wind, fire, and earth, the four points on a compass, the four sides of a square?*

Four is of the material world where we live.

I prefer seven, he decided. *For music. The seven notes that make a symphony.*

The weathered face changed with delight. *Sí. Music is made from the spiritual three and the material four,* she said, as if this made perfect sense.

Juan Pablo smiled at the memory. Rocio was right. His abuela was not really gone; it was just that now she manifested in his mind, popping into being with the slightest reminder of her magical thinking.

Was she with her Sky People now?

He understood it didn't matter because she would always arrive back with memories. He had only to think of her to bring her back. It was as if thoughts of her formed a velvet bridge to the spiritual realm.

He closed his eyes and felt her love pouring over him.

Your mother often helps you with your music, she said once, when he at last had perfected a piece.

Does she? Was she helping me just now?

His abuela nodded.

It was odd, too, because, like at that moment, he often felt an external intelligence guiding him when he played, especially difficult pieces.

The Sky People are often responsible for great ideas and wonderful art.

Was his musical success aided by his mother? Or was it his own intuition, his own unfolding talent?

What if the Sky People were real?

Finding courage from this idea, he slowly emerged from his hiding place, greeted by a bright sun and the soothing sounds of the forest. A wind rustled through the trees. Birds called from the trees above. The hum of a nearby beehive reached him. Cautiously, he started back up the hill, stopping every ten paces to listen.

He finally reached the meadow. One look and he saw it was all clear. He made a quick dash to the other side and soon found his way to the tepee.

"JP."

He fell into Rocio's embrace.

CHAPTER FIVE

Two days later, after a hundred whispered conversations and plans made and abandoned based on the sound of helicopters or men searching, something had changed. Rocio was reading the first Hunger Games book for the second time. Reading was the only thing that softened her fear of what was happening. Just as the only thing that distracted him from thoughts of the Hunter was playing music in his mind.

For long periods the music stole his fear like magic.

Musicians and other artists are the most fortunate people on earth.

We are? Juan Pablo asked.

You can always escape any unpleasant reality into a beautiful one. What a gift.

He started with the simplest pieces in his repertoire. Imagining he played before a large audience, he heard and felt every note. He noticed he played the most difficult pieces much better in his imagination than he did when actually playing. He finished with the most difficult of Paganini's violin concertos, a piece he played brilliantly in his mind, but not so well in reality.

Just as he was trying to figure out what, exactly, had changed, he noticed Rocio's interested stare. "Why are you staring at me like that?"

She reached a hand to knock back a stray lock of his too-long, curly hair.

He knew that smile.

He was amazed to discover they were bored. After all that had happened to them. That was another miracle.

"Your lips are like a girl's."

And they were, too, smooth and full and beautiful like a girl's.

He gave her back her smile and lifted onto his side to stare at her. "And you have feet like a boy's."

She used these to kick him. He pretended it hurt.

"I never told you this," she continued, "but one time, while you were playing at the plaza, I overheard an American couple comment on how handsome you were."

"Really." Skeptical and amused both. "Americans are well known for their poor vision. Was this the problem? Had they lost their glasses?"

Rocio's laughter sounded like music. She punched his shoulder. Then, "Elena always said your green eyes meant you had magic."

"Rocio," Juan Pablo rolled those green eyes with vexation, laughing at her. "You are acting strange." Yet, still she stared at him. "Are you still thinking of my lips?"

She nodded. "I was wondering . . . well, I was wondering if you ever want to kiss me."

Juan Pablo's smile grew. "You must want me to kiss you."

She shrugged, pretending indifference. "Maybe."

"Ah," he replied, "you will have to beg me."

He enjoyed the startled look that changed her face, followed quickly by an outraged yelp. She socked him hard in the arm. He caught her arms easily and pinned them to either side of her head. "Go ahead, beg me to kiss you."

This was greeted with a peal of laughter. "Never," she vowed. "Never—"

It was as far as she got. He suddenly did want to kiss her. Even stranger was the realization he had always wanted to kiss her, but had been waiting for the right moment. Waiting for this moment.

"What are you waiting for?" she whispered.

"It will be our first kiss. I want to do it right."

"Do it like in the movies," she suggested.

"Like this," he first asked as he lowered his head and pressed his lips to hers. Several minutes passed and it came as a surprise, what all the poets were talking about. When he finally lifted up, Rocio's eyes were still closed and a dreamy, dazed look sat next to some small alarm as well.

"Do you like that, Rocio? Should I kiss you again?"

She managed to recover enough to shake her head.

"Why not?"

"I think I am too young."

He supposed this was true. He rolled onto his back and stared up at the apex of the tepee. For a long moment they said nothing. "Rocio?"

"Yes?"

"Will you promise me to let me know when you are not too young?"

Her eyes found him again and she smiled. "I promise, Juan Pablo."

A second startling realization reached him as they lay there in companionable silence, thinking, no doubt, of a future promised to each other. The helicopters had not returned from the morning search. The men who had followed the trail out had all returned yesterday afternoon. There had been no men this morning either. They only had two bottles of almond milk left; they needed to escape as soon as possible.

"What?"

"Listen."

After a moment, she said, "I don't hear anything."

"Exactly. The helicopters haven't returned. I think it is safe."

They knew they had to get started before their thirst and hunger became the enemy. They formed a plan. Juan Pablo would check the meadow while Rocio packed. They still had five, almost six hours of daylight left. They would hike until darkness and then find a sheltered place in the woods to spend the night.

Juan Pablo emerged into the sunlight. He stopped, listening for any sounds before moving on. He made his way quietly to the meadow. He leaned against the trunk of a tall pine and soaked in the familiar sight. A bowl of blue sky arched overhead. Thousands of butterflies still floated in the afternoon sun. In small clusters, the beautiful winged creatures alighted against tree branches, gently fanning their wings. He drew a deep breath and hurriedly traveled the perimeter of the meadow until he could see down to the town.

A small salamander sunned itself on a rock, but no one and nothing moved. No new activity. He turned back to the tepee.

Once inside, he said, "It is all clear in town. I think I can refill the water bottles. We might need it."

Rocio looked at the four empty bottles. "Wait." She handed him one bottle and she took the other. They drained the contents into empty stomachs. He gathered all the bottles to refill. "Use this bag." She passed him one of Elena's shopping bags. "Be careful," she said.

Nodding at this, Juan Pablo took the bag with the empty bottles and ducked outside again. He half ran, half walked to the meadow, and after the briefest of glances, he darted across. Hidden by the forest again, he gave thanks to the trees for their cover as he rushed down the trail to the edge of town. Butterflies followed him overhead, occasionally alighting on his head and shirt. He took it as a good omen.

He paused at the edge of town. Nothing stirred. Without people and cars and noise, the town looked like the set of a movie, not real. His house was first before the forest. As he approached, he knew at a glance it was empty. He raced to the back window and looked inside. He saw his abuela's empty cot, the small table sitting beneath the window. Bottles lay broken beneath the window, their contents spread over the floor. Just a few bottles remained on the shelves. Drawers were opened, their contents scattered over the floor as well, along with sheet music and dozens of paperbacks. His abuela always kept things so neat and tidy. He was glad she would never see this.

He carefully opened the back door and made his way to the sink. Broken glass crunched beneath his sneakers. He turned on the water and began filling the bottles. Once done, he looked around the room, knowing this was the last time for a long time and trying to think if there was anything he would miss.

His abuela kept money in the pocket of an old coat in case of an emergency, so he made his way to the clothes closet. He rifled through the pants and cotton shirts, drawing in the familiar scent. He brought a sleeve to his face and took a deep breath—lavender and rosemary.

He dropped to the floor, pulling the shirt with him. He tried to choke back his grief, and buried his face in the cloth, calling her name through his tears. "Abuela, Abuela . . ."

He felt the warm comfort of her love in answer. He first thought he must be imagining it, but no. It was as if love were a physical thing.

He suddenly remembered the first time he mastered "Ode to Joy."

His abuela applauded with that very emotion.

It is such a powerful manifestation of joy. Your mother felt it, too; it was always our favorite music.

Yes, he had agreed. *Joy and also love, the two best feelings in the world.*

She had laughed at this. *Love is not a feeling, Juan Pablo.*

It isn't? But . . . but I feel it.

Love causes emotions, lots of them, but it is not an emotion. Love is an energy, the strongest force on earth, just as it is in the spiritual realm. In fact everything in the spiritual realm has a meaningful manifestation in our material world and nothing is more meaningful or powerful than love.

He suddenly felt warm. The sweet scent of rosemary and lavender seemed to swirl around him. His eyes closed as his heart lifted.

It was his abuela's love all around him . . .

Te amo, Abuela . . .

He didn't know how long he sat there or how long he would have sat there, but abruptly he became aware of a buzzing in his ears, a strange sensation, like a warning. He stood up again. He found her orange parka—orange was her favorite color, in celebration of the butterflies—and felt for the hidden inside pocket.

Fifty pesos, a windfall. He shoved the money into his pocket and turned to go.

But there was one more thing.

His abuela's photo album, photos taken before phones.

His gaze came to his abuela's bureau. They had left her clothes, but apparently rifled through her jewelry drawer. He peered inside. She had been wearing her plain gold wedding band when they buried her and she had nothing of value after that. He spotted her beaded butterfly pin among the few trinkets left. A gift from a little girl whose life-threatening seizures she had stopped many years ago, it had been a treasure to his abuela. He slipped it into his pocket and opened the bottom drawer where she kept the photo album along with her winter scarves.

He brushed aside the colorful collection of shawls and wraps.

The photo album was gone. Thankfully, he had all the pictures of his mother and abuela on his iPad, plus a hundred pictures of him and Rocio as children.

Why would they take someone's old pictures?

A lone picture had fallen out, one he'd never seen before. It was as if his abuela had left it for him. In the familiar space of the meadow, his beautiful mother stood alongside a tall American-looking man.

Juan Pablo studied the stranger in the photo. Why had he never seen this photo before? Was it his father? If so, he didn't look Mexican at all. The man was tall and thin, wearing Levi's and a work shirt. Sunglasses covered his eyes. He had an oval face, dark hair, and a huge smile, but there was nothing familiar in his features.

A butterfly floated in from the outside. The winged creature flew straight out the door, not really fluttering. More like a warning.

The second warning . . .

His gaze shot to the front door. Footsteps approached. In the next instant, he grabbed the water bottles and raced outside. He ducked into the small garbage enclosure alongside the house and knelt down. Holding perfectly still, he forgot to breathe.

A man entered the house.

There were no sounds at first, as if the man stood there studying the mess made of their home. Cigar smoke wafted outside from the house. Glass crunched beneath boots with each slow and deliberate step. Silence followed, so complete that Juan Pablo imagined he could hear the smoke moving through the stilled air.

What was the man looking at?

The man stepped outside. He couldn't see the man, but he imagined the man stared at the view of the mountain and forest behind the house. The pungent scent of his cigar swirled away in the breeze.

Could this be the man they called the Hunter?

"Juan Pablo *Venesa*."

Juan Pablo almost toppled upon hearing his name. He didn't move, and for several tense moments he was afraid he had been found out, but no. Nothing happened. The man remained staring out.

The man knew his name.

How did they know it was him? He tried to reason, to think how this happened. He couldn't imagine, until—

The vague memory of the video shot on the patio popped into his mind. They would know where the poison had come from after the search of the houses. They needed only to have asked any one of El Rosario's families to get his name. As if to answer his mounting terror, a low chuckle sounded.

"It is only a matter of time, mi amigo . . ."

Juan Pablo's hands flew to his mouth to stop his gasp. Kneeling there, terrified, he fully expected to be discovered.

The man finally returned inside. Glass smashed beneath the unhurried steps, which spoke of an unnatural confidence, as if he had all the time in the world. The front door opened and closed again.

The boots disappeared down the street.

Juan Pablo guessed what color they were.

He ducked past the back door and darted into the forest. Moving cautiously, in case any eyes were upon the mountain trail, he made his way from one tree to the next until he finally reached the tepee.

"JP, what took so long?"

He started to tell Rocio, but something cautioned him. They had been through so much. They didn't need to worry about the strange man looking through his house, did they? Just another bandito searching for them.

"My house," he shook his head. "They went through everything, all of Abuela's things. It is a mess."

Within minutes, they stood outside the tepee and weighted with their packs, they took their first steps on the long journey to freedom. As always, the air was thick with the sweet scent of the surrounding forest. Butterflies circled overhead. They first kept to the trees, moving furtively as they circumvented the meadow to reach the trail.

The tall oyamel fir trees rose on either side of the trodden path and provided welcome shade from the warm afternoon sun. The trail rose up for about a kilometer. Juan Pablo and Rocio both knew this part; they had been up to the top three or four times with friends. They walked in silence, practically tiptoeing, but still moving as fast as they could, looking back every few steps, as if at any moment they would be spotted.

Two anxious gazes darting this way and that.

The trail finally began to flatten. Trees shot straight up in search of the sun. The butterflies began to thin out. Their breathing eased, but they still moved quickly.

In this way, they made steady progress.

Occasionally clearings interrupted the shade and the long arms of the sun reached down to them. Fewer butterflies collected in these clearings. Their numbers seemed to diminish with each step.

"We are going fast, don't you think?"

"If you can keep up with me, we will reach the road in no time."

"Me?" Juan Pablo asked, hiding the burst of joy brought by Rocio's comment. He too would pretend to be normal. "Keep up with you? I am going so slow, to help you keep up."

"But I'm going slow for you."

"I have always been faster than you."

"In your dreams. I am much faster."

They laughed at this lie. Juan Pablo adjusted his pack and violin in front and offered to carry her. Rocio leapt onto his back, as she always had, and he happily carried her for the next kilometer.

"What was that?" Rocio asked in a whisper.

Juan Pablo set her on her feet. "What?"

She pointed up ahead. "I think I heard something."

Juan Pablo took her hand and moving stealthily, they hid behind a grouping of trees. With the sinking sun to their right, the shadows darkened and stretched. The still air amplified the quiet as they waited and listened. He heard his own heartbeat, but also Rocio's coupled with the sound of her short, frightened breaths. They waited maybe five minutes, but nothing happened.

"I think it is clear," Juan Pablo finally whispered.

She nodded slowly. Now spooked, they made their way back onto the trail and continued walking. As the light faded, their heightened senses imagined boots closing in from in front and behind. Rocio suddenly grabbed him and she stopped.

"Rocio, there is no one coming."

She waited a moment before realizing they were safe. "JP, can we stop? I need to rest."

Juan Pablo searched their surroundings for a safe place. He made out a large boulder and some oak brush beneath the trees some fifty meters from the path. He pointed. "Over there."

They made their way to the spot. On the other side of the boulder, they shrugged out of their packs and collapsed to the ground. He and Rocio removed one of their bottles of water.

"We should only have half. For now," Rocio instructed.

"Suit yourself," Juan Pablo replied. "I'm having the whole thing."

"You'll be sorry," Rocio told him.

The warm water slid down Juan Pablo's throat. He tried to stop halfway, but it seemed to only tease his great thirst. He took another big gulp. Rocio watched and suddenly smiled. She took a big gulp too.

"You drank more than half already," Juan Pablo pointed out.

"Maybe I changed my mind," Rocio said, without admitting she was wrong. "I'm starving, too," she said.

Juan Pablo only realized how hungry he was after he drank the whole bottle. He nodded. "Me, too."

Rocio, who seemed to be in charge of the food for some reason, carefully withdrew the tortillas and the peanut butter and using only her finger, she spread the golden paste over two tortillas. This was torn in half. She handed him half.

Juan Pablo never tasted anything so delicious. He could eat ten of them. They ate two more.

Rocio's gaze swept the surrounding forest. "This looks like a good place to stay the night?"

Juan Pablo shook his head. "I think we can hike another two or three kilometers before complete darkness. Then find a place to sleep. We just might make it out by nightfall tomorrow. Besides, my abuela always said night vision was the first thing you lose as you get older. They will need flashlights now, and we don't. We can spot them coming a mile away in the dark."

To Juan Pablo's surprise, Rocio agreed. "That makes sense."

Juan Pablo placed the water back in his pack and stood up, brushing the dirt from his jeans. They hiked another two kilometers, more slowly now in the pending dark. When at last even Juan Pablo couldn't walk any further, they used the phone's light to find a place to sleep. Not far from the trail, they settled on a spot hidden behind a thick cluster of trees. Rocio made him use the light to make certain there were no spiders.

This was the only useful thing the phone could do. They both had realized they could not call anyone. If Rocio's mother knew what was happening, she'd fly in to Mexico City and knowing Rocio's headstrong mom, she would singlehandedly take on the whole lot of banditos. Neither of them saw a happy ending if Rocio's mom learned of the unfolding danger. Even if they all somehow survived, because of the restrictions placed on Mexicans wanting to emmigrate, she would not be allowed back into America. There would be no tuition for medical school and Leonardo would lose his place there.

Still, as soon as they were safe at Rocio's uncle's house, Rocio would call her mother and tell her what had happened to them, that Elena and her father had died.

Rocio went from hopeful to frightened because of the darkness
. . .

After eating the last of the cereal and drinking another bottle of water, they laid down.

Aching muscles, fatigue, and more tired than they ever had been—all of which made for a good thing. They were so tired it didn't matter how uncomfortable they were or that the ground poked them every which way. They lay down side by side, staring up through the trees. Distant stars laced the velvet sky, the panorama interrupted only by the canopy of treetops. Unseen animals scurried into the bushes. An owl hooted nearby. Juan Pablo started to close his eyes on the stars and the soft sound of Rocio's breathing.

"Juan Pablo," Rocio whispered.

"Yes?"

"Thank you for saving me. You were so brave. I'll never forget it."

The rare compliment from Rocio made his heart sing, but he wondered if it was true. Was he brave? He certainly did not feel brave. Ever since the banditos, he felt mostly scared. He'd like to think he was brave, but he had only done what he had to do to save the people he loved.

Maybe that's what bravery was.

"I don't know what would have happened if you—"

"No, don't think of it," Juan Pablo stopped her, reaching for her hand and squeezing it. "It's over. I would go mad if I thought about what might have happened to you, but we don't have to think of this ever again. We're going to get out of here. We'll soon be safe at your uncle's house."

They fell silent for a long moment, before he thought of Sophia, Rocio's mother in Arizona. "Your mom will be so worried."

She nodded. "And sad. She loved my abuelo and Elena very much."

A rising half-moon spread light over the forest.

Holding Rocio's hand as they drifted off to sleep, Juan Pablo studied the darkened shadows cast in the moonlight. He remembered the first time he became aware of the haunting stillness of the forest, the imperfect quiet here.

Juan Pablo, do you hear the music? his abuela had asked.

He had listened with his eyes on the sea of green. An evocative vibration sang into the stilled air. *What is it, Abuela?*

The music of the forest. It is a magnificent giant creature, the forest, humming with life.

What do you mean, creature? He didn't understand the use of the English word.

People tend to see individual trees, but they are not individuals. They are connected at their roots; they are one great being, singing with life.

He listened to the music now.

People are like that, too, only very few grasp the connection to each other. This is why what you do to one, you do to all . . .

CHAPTER SIX

Juan Pablo watched the butterflies begin disappearing until only a barren sky remained. Darkness fell and the sky turned into a murky blackness. From far away, his abuela called out a warning as he and Rocio walked through the darkness. Someone was following them. They started running . . .

The man with the red boots was gaining . . .

Juan Pablo woke with a start and opened his eyes to dawn's light.

Reality played in a nightmare. The trouble was the nightmare was real.

He looked over at Rocio still sleeping soundly.

A fairly large spider, one the size of his thumb, gently walked through Rocio's hair and he reached over and let it crawl onto his hand, lifting it safely away from his sleeping friend.

Understandings of their difficulties piled up as they finally made their way back to the trail and began walking. First, they discovered sore muscles and tired legs. They also needed a shower. But they discovered what all frightened people discover; fear produces an almost supernatural energy. They ignored their aches, hunger, and fatigue to push ahead.

Rocio had combed her hair down the middle and tied the two pigtails with three bands each. She had started to braid her hair, but he had protested. He could never look at braids the same way again. They would forever remind him of an unknown young girl's terrible fate.

As they headed out, making good, steady progress, the landscape gradually changed. The trail took downward turns, interrupted by less-steep inclines. They finally passed the tree line. Boulders and scrub brush began littering the hilly landscape—that was all. Eventually all the trees vanished.

The day warmed with each step. Warm turned to hot and sometime after noon, with maybe ten kilometers still to go, the sun began to beat unrelentingly upon them. He and Rocio tied their shirts over their heads for shade. Juan Pablo felt the sun hit his black jeans like a fire on coals. Perspiration trickled over his bare chest and down his neck.

"All I can think about is how thirsty I am," Rocio mumbled.

Juan Pablo would have added their favorite English word, *ditto*, but even saying it seemed like too much effort.

They each had one bottle left. They had to make it last.

They marched on in the sun.

Mountains rose behind them. While vertical cliffs shot up to the sky on one side, the trail became a flat plane surrounded by hills on the other. With each step Juan Pablo could do nothing to escape thoughts of water. Normally, the weight of his violin did not register, as if indeed it had become a part of him, but he felt it now. Sweat fell in tiny rivulets from his face.

He tried to think of something besides water . . .

Music. He forced his thoughts to music. He began imagining playing Bach's Double Violin Concerto in D Minor, a most difficult piece, one he had mastered only in his mind, but fell far short of even adequate in reality. For a millimeter maybe two, the pounding torture of the sun disappeared beneath a symphony of music. He had just reached the second movement when a butterfly floated dreamily across their path.

He stopped, watching the delicate creature dance leisurely across the trail toward the cliffs.

Follow the butterflies . . .

Dragging her feet, Rocio stared zombie-like at the ground as she stumbled on.

The orange and black creature disappeared behind the towering cliff.

He lifted his shirt to shield the sun from the view. If he squinted against the light just so, he could see the narrowest of paths reaching around the cliff. Probably an old Indian path. Indians used to live here hundreds of years ago, after the Aztecs and before the Spaniards.

"Rocio," he called out. "Look."

Stopping, Rocio cupped her hand over her eyes, studying where he pointed. "What?"

"I don't know. I'm going to look."

"Wait. No. We can't be wasting energy exploring—"

Too late. Juan Pablo climbed up the incline. Not a real path, but more a slight opening in the scrub brush. It disappeared behind the cliff.

Rocio scrambled to catch him.

Juan Pablo stopped as the path rounded the side of the cliff. The sudden shade felt like a cool cloth to his hot head. About fifty kilometers down, a cluster of tall reeds crowded in a circle the size of a house. What struck him where he stood was the color. Green. The color of life—or in this case, water.

Rocio came up behind him.

"I bet there's water there." He turned to the cliff. "Look. You can see where there used to be a waterfall."

"It's dry now," Rocio said, eyeing the climb down with weariness.

"I'm going to look."

He removed his violin and pack, and set these against the cliff's shaded wall. He half slid, half hopped down the steep incline. From above, Rocio watched him disappear in the green reeds.

The next sounds were shot straight from heaven.

A bark of triumphant laughter followed by a splash.

Rocio laughed, too, as she dropped her pack.

The girl was already sliding down the side of the cliff. She pushed away the reeds and confronted a glorious sight.

Juan Pablo swimming in a dark and deep pool of water the size of the plaza. The cliff and reeds completely shaded it. They needed no invitation.

"A gift from the butterflies," Juan Pablo said before diving down into the cool, dark depths.

With laughter, Rocio joined him.

It was probably not wise to drink this water, but their great thirst had squeezed out any semblance of wisdom. Clothes were soaked and then left to dry over the tops of the rocks. Time disappeared as they indulged in the heaven-sent gift. It was hard not to make much noise as they dove and swam to the depths, holding their breath for long minutes, but if smiles made sounds, the noise would be a roar.

Eventually their sore muscles and tired limbs found relief as they floated on their backs. Rocio stared up at the arch of blue sky, but Juan Pablo studied her long hair circling her head and lit by sunlight like a great fan.

A pair of white birds flew overhead, their wings flapping in a slow rhythmic reach against the sky.

"Do you think our abuelos are watching us now?"

"Yes," she answered. "I am imagining their love pouring down on us."

"I never told you what my abuela said about you."

"What?"

"Remember that day you came over and busted into my room without knocking?"

"You were so mad."

Juan Pablo laughed, remembering. "After you left, I complained, *Rocio just opens my door and walks inside like it is her room. She was* mixing potions and at first she didn't say anything. *Yes, Rocio is a door opener.* I asked her, *What do you mean?* and she told me, *Rocio will be a great teacher. I am seeing science and math. She will open doors for many bright young minds.*

A look of wonder lifted Rocio's face. "Did she really say that?"

Juan Pablo assured her that she had.

For several minutes she considered this as they floated peacefully in the water, staring up at the empty sky. He thought it could be true; because of the Khan Academy, he and Rocio were many grades ahead in math. She did love watching his abuela's science shows on TV.

"It is a beautiful dream, becoming a teacher. If only we can get to America and we can go to a university someday."

Juan Pablo imagined studying music at a university; it would indeed be a dream come true.

The two white birds flew back, circled, and zoomed off, interrupting his revelry.

"We have to go, too," Juan Pablo realized.

Revived and refreshed, they emerged from the pond's cool depths. Armed with full water bottles, they fitted their packs on now-cool shoulders. Still dripping wet, Juan Pablo started for the trail.

He was thinking his abuela was right. She was always right.

Follow the butterflies. They will not lead him wrong.

A loud buzzing in his ears sounded a different note. He looked across the vista and stopped dead in his tracks.

A lone man walked on the trail toward the mountain, his back to them.

Juan Pablo's hand snaked out, stopping Rocio. He pressed into the cliff to shield himself in the shadows. Rocio did the same. Neither said a word, but their hearts leapt and pounded against their chests.

Juan Pablo felt the danger this man presented from the tips of his toes to the roots of his hair. Yet, he looked like any other man. Average height, neither tall nor short, he wore a tan cowboy hat, a gray buttoned shirt, Levi's, and red boots. A saddlebag was slung over his shoulder. He puffed an unlit cigar.

The same man who had been in his house.

The man suddenly stopped. He stood stock-still, as if sensing something. He turned around slowly. His hat came off to shield his view from the sun as he surveyed the desolate surroundings.

He paused for a long moment before returning his hat to his head and continuing on.

They remained like that for nearly a half-hour. The man had long since disappeared, heading up the way they had just come. They slowly, silently made their way down to the trail. They moved quickly now.

They needed to get somewhere safe.

Darkness came fast.

Exhaustion defined them. Every muscle ached and throbbed and demanded rest, but there seemed no place safe to sleep. Nothing but rocky desert terrain in all directions. They had to keep going. Juan Pablo thought if he stopped, he'd never get up again.

The stars shone bright in the arch of sky above. A half moon rose over the eastern horizon. He wondered if his grandmother was with his mother now, and if all this time, his mother, too, was sending him love from the sky. He wondered if they could help them more than the butterflies or if they could direct the butterflies to help them. Or could they do nothing? Maybe they couldn't even see them.

What, he wondered, were the rules the Sky People followed?

"We must be getting close," Rocio said.

"How much juice is left in your phone?" Juan Pablo asked.

Rocio stopped and found her phone in the pocket of her backpack. "Seventeen percent."

"How long will the light last?" he asked.

Rocio shrugged. "Maybe an hour?"

"We should just sleep alongside of the trail here."

"Let's use the light until it goes out," Juan Pablo said. "If we are close, it would be better to go around the roadblock at night."

"Good thinking. Okay. Let's go."

Rocio turned on the flashlight and they continued on. Not for long. They traveled another quarter of a mile before they heard it. The distant sound of music. The same booming noise the banditos had played that terrifying night at the cantina.

"That's them. The roadblock set up to catch us."

They exchanged looks of desperate alarm.

"We have to go around." Juan Pablo pointed, whispering urgently, "this way. We need to be on this side, going toward Guadalajara, right?"

Rocio nodded obliquely. The other way eventually led to Mexico City. They could catch a bus to her brother's house from Guadalajara, but that was over sixty or seventy kilometers away. They had not figured out how they would get to Guadalajara. They couldn't walk, that was for sure.

"How much light is left?"

Rocio checked. "Nine percent, maybe a half-hour."

Rocio aimed it as they stumbled over the harsh desert terrain.

Not fifty meters away, the light illuminated a ravine. First Rocio and then Juan Pablo knelt down, attempting to slide. Just before he slipped, something caught his eye. A tiny red dot floated eerily from the trail behind them.

"Look," he whispered. "What is it?"

"What?" Rocio whispered. "I don't see anything?"

"Quick," Juan Pablo whispered urgently. "Kill the light."

Rocio clicked off the phone light.

They stood motionless, staring into the darkness. The tiny red dot approached at a leisurely pace. It was the Hunter with the red boots. Juan Pablo was sure of it. He was returning to the roadblock, his cigar appearing as a tiny red dot moving eerily in space.

Despite the warm, still night, a chill raced down his spine as he watched the steady progress of the red dot dancing down the trail.

The man passed the spot they had just left. He walked no more than ten paces when the red dot turned in their direction.

"Duck," Rocio whispered.

A strong flashlight suddenly swept across the landscape. Back and forth, twice, before moving in slow motion over the darkened space.

Juan Pablo's mind raced. The man must have hiked the trail all day. Yet at some point, he figured they had passed him somewhere and he turned around. How did he know? He tried to think if they left anything behind, but he couldn't think of anything.

It was like the man had a gift. Like his abuela, only instead of helping people, this man used it to track people.

The light finally disappeared. They waited like that, crunched into frightened balls in the ravine for maybe fifteen more minutes. Slowly, they emerged on the other side. They could not risk the light now. They moved as quickly as they could, aiming west of the roadblock and slightly south, hoping to find the road before the banditos found them.

Holding hands for safety, they put one foot in front of the other over the rough ground. The change came suddenly; there came a slight dip, and once over it, they were walking on pavement. "The road. We're on it," Juan Pablo marveled.

They looked to the left in search of a sign of the roadblock but saw nothing but darkness.

"What should we do now?" Rocio asked.

"We should walk alongside the road, but far enough away so no one coming can spot us."

"I can't walk anymore," Rocio said.

"We will sit and wait then for daylight."

"JP, I'm scared."

"Me too," he said, realizing they had no options now. What would they do? Walk fifty-plus miles in broad daylight with no food left? That would never work.

Abuela, this problem has no solution, he remembered complaining once about a piece of music he struggled with.

If a problem has no good solution, then it is best to decide not to have the problem.

They only made it about twenty paces from the road when in the far distance, headlights approached. They both fell to the ground, crouching there as they watched. Another set of headlights followed the first.

One black SUV after another.

A large black Cadillac car passed next.

They didn't speak until the red lights disappeared altogether.

"I bet that was the men at the roadblock," Juan Pablo said.

"It must be," Rocio said. "Does that mean it's safe now?"

"I think so," Juan Pablo said as they sat up.

"That was so close," Rocio said.

"Too close. We just made it."

"Want some water?"

They drank a bottle, as if to celebrate.

"We might as well sleep here," Juan Pablo realized.

"Might as well, I guess," Rocio said.

They started to arrange their backpacks when another set of headlights appeared in the distance. These were unlike the others— yellow and placed close together. They moved very slowly down the road. "I wonder what it is."

"Not banditos?"

Juan Pablo shook his head. Somehow he knew it was not the narco-traffickers. "Maybe whoever it is will give us a ride to Guadalajara."

Grabbing their packs, they moved toward the road. The headlights drew closer and closer until he saw that it was an old truck. Swallowing his hesitation, Juan Pablo moved out onto the road and waved.

The truck came to a stop. The engine died.

"You go," Rocio said.

"Me?"

"Make sure they look nice," Rocio said, practically pushing Juan Pablo toward the truck as she held back.

Taking a deep breath, Juan Pablo approached the driver.

He was surprised to make out a young boy driving a truck. He looked quite a bit younger than himself. A bowl of short dark hair crowned a round, smiling face. A man sat in the passenger side, hidden in the dark. They exchanged a friendly greeting. A sound came from the truck's bed and with a start, Juan Pablo saw several goats huddled in the back.

"We need a ride to Guadalajara."

The boy looked to his father. Juan Pablo could barely make out the older man's features in the dim light, but he had a strong prominent nose, which his grandmother always said was a good sign.

I have never met a stupid person with a fine, large nose. I'm sure they exist, but I have never met one.

He pushed his glasses back up and slowly wiped a bandana across his brow.

"Are you running away, son?"

"No, no. We, well, you see, my friend Rocio, her abuelo had a heart attack and died two days ago."

"Condolences," the father said in a voice of concern.

"Yes, it is very sad for us. He was a good man, a good abuelo. My abuela sent me with Rocio for safety reasons." This was mostly true. "We are trying to reach Rocio's uncle in a village north of Puerto Vallarta. We have money for the bus, but first we must reach Guadalajara. Can you help us?"

That is how Rocio and Juan Pablo found themselves in the back of an old truck, lying on the fresh straw covering the truck bed, their heavy packs on either side to protect them from the four curious goats. The truck slipped into gear and they were off.

Juan Pablo slipped his hand into Rocio's, they closed their eyes, and once again they slept the dreamless sleep of the exhausted.

CHAPTER SEVEN

Juan Pablo knew Rocio was pretty, of course. He could see after all, but he never realized just how pretty she was. She was just Rocio to him, but now sitting in the bus station, waiting for their bus, he noticed the stares of certain men upon spotting her. That man smoking by the lockers. The two teenage boys across from them.

Three times men had approached them and asked if Rocio needed help or wanted a soda or, once, an ice cream. "No, gracias," she replied, and he would take her hand possessively as they hurriedly moved on. She was not safe, even without the man with the red boots looking for them.

They had spent the day exploring the modern and historic city of Guadalajara. Juan Pablo played his violin at the gorgeous plaza at the city center to get money to feed their enormous appetites. He played classical pieces he knew and mixed them up with popular ones. Within two hours, they had nearly 200 pesos. Weighted by their packs, they examined restaurant menus and judged each picture posted on them, searching for the biggest bounty.

It was the best food they had ever had. Giant plates of huevos rancheros, spinach, and potato-stuffed empanadas, tomato juice, and all the water they could drink. Afterward, on the way back to the bus station, they visited the famous Guadalajara Cathedral, where Rocio pretended she was getting married and JP had to be both the priest and the groom. They went to an Internet café so Rocio could recharge her phone and he could recharge his iPad. With the last of the money, they bought a caffe mocha to share.

All day long, homeless children placed stickers on them, reaching out slender arms for a handout: he got a smiley face and a peace sign, while Rocio got a cross and a flower. They had no more money, so Juan Pablo kept giving them packets of milkweed seeds to sell. "Ask for three pesos from Mexicans and twenty pesos from Americans and Europeans," he instructed.

Sipping on the last of their coffee, they waited for the five-thirty bus to Puerto Vallarta. They had seven minutes until boarding. They might have taken an earlier bus, but they realized if they took the last bus instead, they could safely sleep on the seats instead of trying to find a safe place to spend the night in Puerto Vallarta. It was definitely not safe to sleep in the streets.

People-watching through the window, Juan Pablo wondered how a single day, brought about by both tragedy and calamity, could be so much fun.

The red boots appeared on the other side of the terminal window.

Juan Pablo gasped. "Rocio." He said her name in a whisper of fear. "Look."

"What?"

"That's him."

"Who?"

"The bandito looking for us. The red boots."

The man entered the crowded building.

Juan Pablo and Rocio rose simultaneously, dropped their drinks into the garbage, and headed for the bus. Just in time. The driver sat, reading a paper. He had already checked their tickets, so he only nodded as they climbed onboard and took their seats in the back. The bus appeared half full. No one looked at them; the other passengers pretended they were invisible in the way of city people.

"Stay down," Juan Pablo urged.

They crouched down in their seats as two other people boarded. Juan Pablo peeked at the driver, who put down his phone and started the engine.

Minutes felt like an eternity. Juan Pablo peered cautiously above their seats. He searched the terminal, looking for the man with the red boots. He froze upon spotting him at the ticket counter. The clerk nodded, pointing to the bus. The man turned with a start and ran toward them.

"He's coming!"

Rocio almost screamed. The doors shut.

The bus slowly pulled into the road. Juan Pablo watched the man with the red boots stopped just behind the bus. Hands on hips, he stood there as the bus pulled away before he turned and began running to the parking lot.

The bus made its way onto the street.

Juan Pablo sat back. "We lost him, I think."

"You think?"

"I don't know."

He made an anxious study of the cars as the bus moved slowly onto the highway. Rocio still knelt down, both her hands wrapped around his leg, where she buried her face. Juan Pablo noted the cities they passed on the freeway: Tlaquepaque, Tonalá, Zapopan.

Rocio finally sat tensely in her seat at his side.

Juan Pablo stared intently out the window.

He abruptly noticed a black Cadillac driving alongside of the bus on the four-lane freeway. His eyes widened with the fear that it was him—the man with the red boots. The tinted windows offered no sure clue.

"Rocio . . ."

She turned her frightened eyes to the sight. "Is it him?"

"I don't know."

The two watched as the Cadillac kept to the bus's side. The bus moved into the fast lane as the slow lane headed to an off-ramp. The Cadillac fell behind the bus. Juan Pablo stood and looked to the last row of seats across the back of the bus.

Only an old woman slept there, surrounded by shopping bags. Rocio froze and stared straight ahead as Juan Pablo made his way to the back. He cautiously looked out. The Cadillac followed a car length behind the bus. A cracked window from the car allowed the wind to grab smoke, sending it violently into the air.

It was him. The man with the red boots. The Hunter.

"We should get off at the next stop," Rocio said.

"He's following us. He'll catch us."

The back of her hand went to her mouth, as if to stop her panic. "What are we going to do?"

"I don't know. Let me think."

They fell into a tense silence. Every five minutes, Juan Pablo got up and looked out the back window. Returning to his seat beside Rocio, he leaned over, resting his head in his hands, and tried to think of an escape.

"We should tell the bus driver," Rocio said.

Juan Pablo looked over at her, his expression one of confusion. "What can he do?"

"Drive faster."

"Rocio." He rolled his eyes before explaining as if to a very young child. "We are in a bus. He is in a car. Even if the bus driver went faster, a car will always beat a bus."

"You don't know everything, Juan Pablo." She only used his full name when she was mad. "We have to do . . . something."

"That is stupid. It's not going to help."

"If you don't go tell him, I will." She cast him a look that dared him to refuse.

Juan Pablo didn't bother answering. He knew that look. He just sighed and looked away. She was so stubborn.

With a disdainful look back, Rocio rose and boldly marched down the aisle to the driver.

Juan Pablo couldn't hear the conversation, but the driver listened intently to Rocio, whose arms were flying as she described their terrible circumstances. But what exactly was she telling him?

The driver asked the girl a question. She lowered her head and replied.

The driver cursed, then nodded. Rocio's hand touched the driver's shoulder and she was saying *gracias, gracias*. She finally returned to her seat.

"What happened? What did he say?"

"He said he will take care of it."

Right away, the bus began to speed up. They grabbed onto the rail to steady themselves.

"But how?" Juan Pablo asked, his confusion mounting. "Does he think he can outrun the Cadillac? What did you tell him?"

"Everything. That the droguistas killed our abuelos. That we witnessed it and now they want to kill us. That the black Cadillac is one of them. That we are afraid and we don't know what to do." She said in a whisper, "He is very sympathetic. He lost a son to drugs— he thinks he was murdered by them. Then, last year, his sister-in-law was disappeared. His wife is still sick about it, and together, they are trying very hard not to be broken human beings. He said this was the first thing that will help."

Juan Pablo absorbed this in an instant. It seemed there was hardly a person unaffected by the narco-traffickers. Millions of people held hostage at one time or other, in one way or another by this plague of criminals.

Still, how was this going to help them?

"He is going to outrace a Cadillac?"

"That is not his plan."

The bus hit a wind tunnel, swerved, righted itself. Juan Pablo hung on for dear life, terrified now of a crash on top of being caught by the man with the red boots. Most of the passengers were asleep or sat with their eyes closed, but some turned to look out the windows, sensing the dramatic change.

"What is his plan?"

"He knows some police. One is even a cousin. Look." She motioned her head toward the driver. "He is calling them now."

The driver spoke into his cell phone while he sped down the freeway.

"The police. They never stop them—that is the problem."

Rocio shushed him. "You will see."

Juan Pablo managed to stand. Holding on to one seat at a time, he made his way back.

The Cadillac still followed a car length behind, easily keeping up with the fast-moving bus. His mind raced at the same nerve-wracking speed.

Swirling red lights appeared in the far distance.

Closer and closer they came. Two police cars pulled up behind the Cadillac. The Cadillac slowed and moved to the side of the road, boxed in by the circling red lights of the police cars. The bus pulled away.

Juan Pablo made his way to the bus driver who was chuckling merrily.

"You saved us," Juan Pablo marveled.

"That was the most fun I've had driving since I drove the entire Cruz Azul team to Guadalajara."

"But what did you tell the police?"

He shrugged. "I told them a man in a black Cadillac was chasing a beautiful young woman on my bus, that the young woman needed our help."

"Gracias," Juan Pablo said. "Gracias," he repeated, because once wasn't enough.

He fell into the seat beside Rocio, who wore a very pleased smile.

"Sometimes you don't need to ask the Sky People; sometimes a normal person will do."

Juan Pablo had to concede the point.

It took almost an hour before he could take an easy breath. He kept checking, but there was no sign of a black Cadillac or any car following the bus.

His thoughts spun crazily.

He felt the curious buzzing in his ears, like a warning.

A series of startling revelations followed. The man with the red boots was not giving up.

He wanted him, not Rocio. They didn't even know about Rocio.

He considered the issue from every which way, but always came to the same conclusion. He knew what he had to do. He had to save Rocio by leaving her. He would wait until she fell asleep and then get off the bus. She would get to her uncle's house, where she would be safe, while he began the long journey north. Hopefully, the Hunter would not find him. The world was big and he was small, a nobody with a violin. It would be like that other American saying: like finding a tiny thing in a haystack.

And if the Hunter did catch him?

It would only be him. Rocio would be safe.

Juan Pablo said nothing of his plan. Rocio would be upset when she woke and found him gone, but he knew she would understand. He would text her as he made his way north. Someday, when it was safe, they would be reunited.

He had to do it. There was no other way.

Still afraid, too, Rocio held his hand as they sat, staring out the window, half expecting the Cadillac to manifest at their side. Hours passed, marked only by the occasional passing of cities and towns and endless miles of farmland. Darkness settled over the landscape and the view out the window became a blur of red, white, and yellow lights interrupting long stretches of darkness. Most of the passengers seemed to be sleeping, while Rocio's fear finally eased a bit. Desperate to distract her and make her feel better, he took out his iPad and clicked on one of her favorite games: SimCity.

He hid his sadness from her as they built a beautiful house. It was two stories, white with a picket fence. Rocio loved the huge garden and small barn stocked full of animals. They scored enough points to finally add a dog. Rocio studied the pictures of available pets with a strange intentness, as if it were a real choice instead of just a game.

She finally stopped on one that looked almost like Tajo.

Juan Pablo watched her eyes wet with tears. The picture showed a dog just a little taller than Tajo, with his straight, gray ears, white muzzle, and gray and white curly hair. His hand came over Rocio's, and he squeezed it, as he remembered the horror from the night that changed everything.

Shifting, Rocio rested her head in his lap. He let his fingers comb lightly through her long hair. The realization suddenly occurred to him—there was no one alive that he loved more than this girl.

The thought gave him the courage to do what he had to do.

He leaned back and closed his eyes, but his heart pounded as he waited until she fell into a troubled, restless sleep.

Then he sent her his first text: *I cannot go with you to your uncle's house. They are after me. If I am gone, you will be safe. I will text all the way to California. You are my best friend, Rocio, and I love you. Think of me whenever you see a butterfly.*

Then he quietly rose and told the bus driver to let him out at the next stop.

CHAPTER EIGHT

Juan Pablo kept his gaze down on the ground as he made his way through the brightly lit boulevards of Puerto Vallarta. Tall buildings lined both sides of the crowded street. He passed bustling restaurants, shops, nightclubs, and a movie theater. Strolling couples, in twos and fours, ignored the beggars strategically positioned outside the fanciest restaurants and hotels. Restaurant hawkers called out to pedestrians, offering great deals on seafood and steak dinners and margaritas. A street musician serenaded a busy corner with a Spanish version of "Time After Time."

Juan Pablo stopped to listen. He was not the only person either. A crowd of ten deep formed around the enchanting singer. People began dropping pesos and dollars into the singer's open guitar case.

Hope came from the sight. He moved on. The pretty music faded, swallowed up in the noise of a busy street.

The boulevard opened to a space between buildings that led to closed beachwear shops and a bit further on, the beach. He turned off the street. The relentless noise, honking cars, sirens, and shouts of people fell away to the soft sounds of the sea. Stepping onto the sand, he marveled at the night sky arching over the vast black space of the ocean.

Juan Pablo set down his pack and violin and sat down, still staring at the distant stars. At one point he laid his head on his backpack, willing the soothing sound of the waves to lure him into a deep, dream-filled sleep.

Dreams of Rocio's laughter interrupted by gunfire.

Dreams that turned into nightmares of being chased.

He opened his eyes to the soft light of dawn stretching over a cloudless sky and the big blue ocean. The sight was a balm for his scorched senses. Mesmerized by the field of blue colors, he felt like he had awoken from a battlefield to find himself on a heavenly shore. He had seen the ocean a million times on TV and in movies, but only once in real life—on a field trip when he had still been in school.

He drew the rich scents deep into his lungs.

Gentle waves lapped at the shore and somehow made a mockery of time. The ceaseless movement beneath the surface hinted at the hidden mystery there—a wholly different world, teeming with life. He felt as if the ocean itself was a living thing.

You do not need a redwood tree to feel small, Abuela . . .

Drawn to the unmistakable magic of the water, he removed his jeans and T-shirt and greeted the day with a splash into the cool waves. Over an hour later, as he dried off in the early morning sun, he thought, reasonably, first things first. He needed enough money to buy a bus ticket to Mazatlán. There he would take the ferry to Baja.

Somehow, someway, he would make it.

Rocio would be safe now at her uncle's house. He drew a deep breath, comforted by the thought, by the idea that he had done the right thing.

Burdened with his violin and pack, and ignoring his hunger, he headed north to the tourist part of town. Apartments and condominiums lined the beachfront property as far as the horizon.

As the sun rose, the blue of the Pacific changed, becoming more jewel-like. He kept walking until the condominiums gave way to hotels. He began looking for the most expensive one.

He stopped on the beach in front of the tallest of the hotels. He sat on the sand to study the place.

Two men lined up beach lounges in neat rows. Each lounge came with a large blue umbrella. People already collected there. A patio restaurant jutted out over the sand. Waiters, wearing neat red and white uniforms in the hot sun, soon appeared with sandwiches and tall drinks.

Finally, a man came by selling kites.

Juan Pablo waited to see if any of the waiters shooed him away. None did.

He smoothed his hair down and drew a deep breath.

He opened his violin case and removed his instrument.

He began to play.

He'd been terrified someone would shoo him away, but instead, after finishing a *Phantom of the Opera* medley (always popular with tourists), a man signaled the waiter to deliver him twenty-five pesos. Two more diners did the same. He opened his violin case so he could play while people tipped him.

The money gave him confidence and he began playing with more assurance. After an hour, he stopped noticing the pesos piling up and he knew only the music. He never stopped to wonder at how easily this happiness came to him.

At the end of the morning, he collected all his money. Seventeen American dollars and 400 pesos. The most he ever made in his life. Stuffing his pockets with the bounty, feeling rich, he took a break to run up the steps to the crowded boulevard. He found a small store, where he reached for a soda, but paused. His abuela wouldn't approve. He reached for an orange juice, water, and an apple instead.

These were greedily devoured.

He returned to his spot and began playing again.

Money piled up even faster in the afternoon once people started drinking.

"Hombre joven, ven aca."

Juan Pablo pieced together the unfamiliar Spanish: *Young man, come here.*

Holding his violin, he climbed the stairs to the patio.

He approached the older woman who had spoken. She wore a pale blue sundress and matching shoes. A kind smile spread across her wrinkled face. "Hola," she said, and then began speaking an animated but incomprehensible Spanish. He listened intently, but he barely understood a word. He listened harder—something about a misbehaving daughter. Her hands flew in all directions, as if she were going to take flight.

Gathering his courage, he interrupted to ask, "Would you mind speaking English?"

Her surprise disappeared in sudden laughter. "No one ever understands my Spanish."

Juan Pablo had no trouble believing this.

She patted the bun made of her gray hair, tiny blue stones wrapped all around the silver mount, glittering in the afternoon sun. Rocio, he knew, would love the old woman's hair decoration.

"What is your name, young man?"

"Juan Pablo."

"You play so beautifully."

"Thank you." He bowed and like any musician, his heart sang with the compliment.

"Juan Pablo, I have a problem, you see. My daughter, my only daughter," she added as an aside, "just decided to get married. This very afternoon! Right here. We all came down together for her cousin's wedding and well, I guess it was contagious. If you can believe that."

Juan Pablo could believe anything, but what did this have to do with him? Why was she telling him of this marriage? He wondered if his hunger was addling his brain.

"Suddenly they cannot wait another day," she said, shaking her head, but laughing, too. "This is so . . . so impulsive of her!" She added again, "You play so beautifully."

"Gracias," he repeated, thinking the old woman didn't make sense in English either.

"Do you know Pachelbel's Canon?"

Juan Pablo could scarcely believe his luck. "Sí. It is one of my favorites. But it is really an orchestral piece. It is not as pretty with just one violin."

"Never mind that. Just play it as best you can."

He struck his bow to the strings and began. As he played, her hands went to her heart and her smile seemed straight from heaven. Once he finished, the diners on the patio began applauding. The woman leaned over and kissed him.

"You were sent from heaven. Now, are you here alone? Are you with anyone I should talk to?"

Juan Pablo started to shake his head, but a waiter appeared suddenly with a tall glass of iced tea. She took the glass in hand and turned back to him. "We have to hurry. It's about to start. This way."

He packed up his case and grabbed his backpack. To his surprise, the waiters did not mind—two of them applauded and bowed as he followed his patron and passed the patio dining area. The tourists at Rosario always seemed to appreciate his music, but never this much.

His cheeks glowed and not from the sun.

She led him inside the cool air-conditioned hotel. The Grand Hotel. He followed her down a spacious hall, decorated with fine chairs, mirrors, paintings, and huge bouquets of flowers. Juan Pablo had never been in such a place, but he had often seen it in movies. He marveled at the opulence.

If only Rocio could be here with him.

The old woman turned into a special room off to the side.

Decorated with pink and white roses, the room opened onto a smaller private patio overlooking the blue Pacific Ocean. One of the waiters, an older, heavyset man, stepped forward and introduced himself. "Lukas here, señor."

"Lukas, find Juan Pablo something more formal to wear?"

"Sí. This way, my young friend."

The waiter bowed. As Lukas led him away, another waiter appeared with a giant chocolate milkshake. This was handed to Juan Pablo. Thanking Lukas profusely, he drank it all at once, followed by a huge glass of water.

Lukas led him to a restroom off to the side of a grand hall. It was a bathroom just for the waiters—one as big as his whole house. He would have liked to explore the hotel, but there wasn't time. The suit jacket Lukas lent him was just a bit too large, but it completed his transformation. For the first time in his life, he felt like a professional musician.

Back at the private patio, he stood nervously in the corner and waited as a small party gathered.

Again, he thought, Rocio would have loved this.

CHAPTER NINE

After purchasing his bus ticket, Juan Pablo found a place on the hard seats. He kept one hand on the wad of cash in his pocket, feeling a dumbfounded astonishment at his windfall. Not only was it enough for a bus ticket and a nice dinner, but it was enough to pay for the ferry to Baja. One day of playing his violin and he was suddenly rich.

Riches and money, his abuela did not believe in such things. He remembered when a very rich family arrived in Rosario and made a huge show of trying to help save the butterflies by purchasing the forest. *How can you purchase a forest?* his abuela had questioned. *How can you own it? Like owning the sky or the ocean—preposterous.* Still it was done and given to the Mexican government for protection from tree poachers. The loggers, the poorest people on earth, chopped down trees and sold the trunks for $2. The trouble was the tree poachers neither knew nor cared if the tree was protected by the government.

The head of the family encountered his abuela's philosophy when he was introduced to her at the ceremony. He made the mistake of explaining his generosity this way: "I have so much and now it is time for me to give back."

That is all very well his abuela had replied, *but why did you have to take so much in the first place?*

The wad of money felt heavy in Juan Pablo's pocket as he remembered this.

Rocio would be at her uncle's house by now. He removed his iPad to check on her and tell her of his good fortune—only to finally see the desperate missive:

Rocio: *Help. My uncle is gone. Someone is in his house. The man with the red boots? I can't see. I am hiding in the alleyway of the next house. I called my uncle's number and someone answers, but they don't say anything. They just breathe.*
JP, I am so scared.
I don't know what to do. I am going to go back to the bus stop, but I have no money for a ticket.
Help me, JP.

Leaping up, Juan Pablo rushed through the busy station until he spotted a Western Union station.

JP: *Is there a Western Union there?*

She must have been staring at her phone, because almost instantly she replied:

Rocio: *Yes.*
JP: *Find out how much a ticket is to Mazatlán. I will wire you the money and meet you at the bus stop when you get off.*
Rocio: *Where did you get money?*
JP: *Long story. Hurry.*

Late that night, exhausted, scared again, Juan Pablo waited two hours for Rocio's bus at the Mazatlán station. He hid in the shadows, hoping no one would notice him. Men and women, all carrying bags and suitcases, hurried onto buses and off, disappearing into taxis or cars in the parking lot. Two policemen, heavily armed, made the rounds. He pretended to play a game on his iPad until they had passed. The police stopped before three women wearing tight, sparkly clothes and teetering on high heels. Laughter erupted from the group. A policeman tapped one of the women with his baton and she stumbled forward, righting herself just before falling. Everyone laughed, even the wronged lady. The police moved on.

Abuela, what is a prostitute?

It is a very sad story.

What had the man with the red boots done to Rocio's uncle?

What would he do to him and worse, Rocio, should they get caught?

He forced these terrifying thoughts out of his mind.

There were dozens of homeless children. If not homeless, then close to it. Ragged clothes, worn shoes or dirty feet, they wore hungry looks of desperation.

You cannot save everyone, this is true, Juan Pablo, his abuela once said. *But this doesn't mean you don't do your best. Sometimes the Sky People will put someone right in front of you and ask you to help.*

A boy, about ten or eleven, was making his way to each garbage can and peering inside. He carried two shopping bags full of plastic bottles. The boy looked at Juan Pablo and offered up a smile. Fear almost made him forget how to respond to this simple greeting, but he forced it and smiled back. The boy fished out his discarded bottle from the nearby bin. He wore grubby, beige pants, a too-big T-shirt, and worn flip-flops. Dirt smudged his lean face and his eyes looked large and hungry, too big for his face.

"How much do you get for a bottle?" Juan Pablo asked.

"Two pesos. I only need two more."

"Two more for what?"

"It's ten pesos to sleep in this alley."

"That's a lot," Juan Pablo said.

The boy shrugged. "Sí, but it is safe there. No one will bother you behind the cantina. Sometimes there is leftover food, too. If the dogs don't get it first." The boy seemed about to invite Juan Pablo, but his eyes locked on Juan Pablo's iPad.

Some people believe money is the root of all evil, his abuela once explained. *It is not. But that is not to say that too much money doesn't pose very serious problems.*

Abuela, wouldn't you say it is better to have that problem than the problem of not enough money?

There is no such thing as not enough money. There is only a problem of not enough sharing.

Juan Pablo reached into his pocket and withdrew fifty pesos. "Here," he said.

The boy's smile was a thing of wonder. "Gracias."

Finally, the yellow and silver bus drove into the spot where the bus driver had told him to wait. The doors opened. Rocio was the first one out.

Juan Pablo dropped his bags as Rocio fell into his arms.

For a long while he just held her slim shape against his; his relief was keen. "I should never have left you. I thought you'd be safer."

She just clung tighter. He felt her shake with tears.

"Come, we need to get out of here."

Rocio nodded as he led her out of the bus terminal. They passed through el Zona Dorada, the Golden Zone—the tourist area of the city. An older homeless boy had warned him that the police picked up unaccompanied minors there and shipped them to orphanages that were "the darkest place on earth, trust me on this, amigo." They made their way quickly past the brightly lit streets, the knickknack shops, a multitude of peddlers, restaurants, and a dozen resort hotels. Rocio watched the passersby with fear now.

She whispered, "What do you think they did to my uncle?"

"I don't know," Juan Pablo replied. "Maybe he is safe somewhere. Maybe he saw the man with the red boots coming and he went vamoose." He dared not offer another maybe.

"Do you think . . . they could have killed him?"

"No, no," he answered as he stopped before a crippled beggar. A buzzing came to his ear, the dim static reminding him of his lost abuela, never far from his thoughts. He reached into his pocket and withdrew three pesos and dropped them in to the beggar's cup.

The man rewarded him with a toothless smile.

"Why would they?" Juan Pablo asked, too scared by the idea of people killing innocents for no good reason, for any reason. "He has done nothing to them."

Yet, he and everyone knew of forty-three college students who disappeared and in the search for them, mountains of human remains had been found. None of these human bones were the forty-three students. Who were they then? No one knew, beyond that they were the legions of the disappeared, people who had been murdered by the drug cartels. They were the sad remains of the innocent, like Rocio's uncle.

This couldn't be happening, it couldn't. "You need to call your mom, Rocio."

Rocio stopped and pulled him into an alleyway. Her lip trembled and she burst into tears as she withdrew her phone to show him. There were twenty-eight calls from her mother. "She must know something is wrong."

"Rocio! Call her and tell her you are okay."

"I left a message that I was safe at my uncle's, that the phone service is down, and that I would call her as soon as I can."

"You need to tell her what happened to us."

"I can't. She would be so scared for us, and for her brother. She'd fly here right off and then what? She would lose her green card and her place in line. We would lose everything."

Rocio's mother had less than a year before she became a citizen, the immigration officer promised. Until then, she could not fly back to Mexico, simply because she would not be allowed back into the United States.

Juan Pablo understood this, but still he knew his abuela would want Rocio's mother to know what was happening to them.

"We need to get to America. Somehow. Many people have done it. We can do it," she said, but without certainty, as if only now confronting the equally daunting and dangerous passage of crossing the border without proper papers. "I will call her when we cross the border and are safe. I will tell her everything then."

Juan Pablo considered this. His abuela always knew when something was wrong. Once, when he was ten, a group of kids kept threatening to beat him up if he didn't "share" his schoolwork. His abuela had seen his fear the second he got home. That's when his abuela got him an iPad so he could take classes online at the Khan Academy, and he had stopped going to school.

Burdened by their packs, he directed her to the cobblestone streets of the old town near the southern end of the peninsula. There were fewer people here and it seemed much safer. The ocean stretched out to the west. The Bahía Dársena channel flowed with the tide on the other side.

They finally found themselves looking up at a beautiful cathedral in the center of the peninsula. From where they stood, they spotted a lighthouse at the southern tip of the long stretch of land cushioned between the ocean and the harbor. Rocio's phone said that the sport-fishing fleet and the Baja ferry building were nearby.

"We should sleep there," Rocio said. "The church will keep us safe."

Juan Pablo agreed. They found a place alongside the enormous building, hidden by the shadows of the steeple. They put sweatshirts on against the cold and kept close to stay warm. Juan Pablo closed his eyes, drawing in the sweet scent of Rocio's shampoo mixed with the rich taste of the ocean.

Still, his thoughts kept returning to the danger surrounding them.

Even in the darkest times, you can choose happiness. You can choose your thoughts . . .

He returned his thoughts to Rocio, close and safe in his arms.

The thought brought him peace. Sleep followed.

CHAPTER TEN

By early morning their carefully considered plans had fallen through.

Juan Pablo and Rocio sat on a bench overlooking the harbor. The morning sun rose over the glass-like surface of the ocean, its warmth chasing away the cold. He drew a deep breath, watching a pelican floating in the bay, a seagull alongside, the unlikely friends as content as his abuela after a healthy birth. He tried to keep this happy thought in his mind.

They tried to decide what to do next. The ferries did not allow children onboard without a guardian. They also only had enough money for one passage. He'd have to play his violin for three or four days to earn enough.

Three or four days of danger, of risking being spotted . . .

Somehow they had to get across the sea to Baja. He silently asked the Sky People for help, just in case it worked again.

They passed an orange juice back and forth while they each ate a banana. Rocio tossed the banana peel into a rusty garbage can before she took out a brush and began combing the tangles out of her long hair.

"Maybe if we ask the ferry captain if we share a bunk? Maybe he would cut the price of passage?"

"We would need to find someone who would pose as our parent—"

Juan Pablo stopped all of a sudden, spotting a butterfly floating by in the new sunlight. He leapt up and grabbed his violin and pack. Rocio dropped her comb in her pack and rushed to follow. Together they chased the flitting creature down the dock. As if distracted, the butterfly drifted aimlessly over a boat. An old man slept on the deck.

"It's a sign," Juan Pablo whispered.

Rocio nodded. They stared, trying to get the courage to wake him.

"He looks really old," Rocio whispered.

The sun had colored the old man's weathered face a dark brown. Wisps of stringy gray hair appeared from beneath a battered old baseball hat and his nose, even from a distance, looked swollen and shone with an unnatural pink. A bottle of whiskey rested in his hands as if he had been afraid to part with it. He wore a torn shirt and ripped, stained white pants, that was all.

The boat did not appear any more promising than the man. The once white paint was now a dingy gray, chipped and as weather-beaten as the old man's face. Fading letters spelled *Catori* on the bow. Juan Pablo racked his brain for a translation but he knew of no such word in either Spanish or English. Both the boat and its captain had lost a battle and given up. The boat hardly looked seaworthy.

Juan Pablo searched for the butterfly for reassurance, but it was nowhere to be seen now. "Should we wake him?"

"You do it."

"Why do I have to do everything?"

"You are the man."

"Ha!" He could scarcely believe this air-thin explanation. "Why are we always equal, except when you want me to do something?"

"Please? I'm afraid he will yell at us."

Sighing, Juan Pablo took a reluctant step forward. "Pardon, señor?"

The man did not stir.

Juan Pablo repeated it in a louder voice.

He still did not stir.

Rocio pantomimed someone drinking a bottle, indicating he was still drunk, sleeping it off. "You're going to have to shake him," she advised.

Drawing a deep breath, Juan Pablo dropped his bags and stepped over the rail onto the boat. "Señor?" He gently shook his shoulder.

The man finally started to wake. Kind of. One large, round brown eye opened.

Juan Pablo introduced himself and Rocio. Another brown eye opened. The two received a surprisingly thorough appraisal. The man's interested gaze lingered on Juan Pablo's violin case before returning to the boy.

"We need to get to Baja."

"You're in trouble." He did not ask a question, but rather stated a fact.

Juan Pablo wondered about the meaning behind the words. Not only did this man understand trouble, but Juan Pablo somehow grasped that the old man would not be adding to theirs. He might not help them, but he would not hurt them. He sensed, too, that this man had so much of his own trouble, it had cloaked him in sadness, the kind of sadness, his grandmother said, that buries the spirit.

He and Rocio exchanged glances before returning their gaze to the man. Juan Pablo nodded. The man looked away, toward the channel opening to the big blue. He stared steadily over this distance, seeming to struggle with some internal battle before turning back to them.

"Someone is chasing you."

A good guess, Juan Pablo supposed. Again he nodded.

"Not a parent or a relative."

Juan Pablo exchanged glances with Rocio again. She looked back at the man and shook her head. Though again, he hadn't really asked a question.

"How did you find me?"

"A butterfly circled your boat," Rocio ventured. "We are from El Rosario, the butterfly sanctuary. We took it as a good sign, like an omen."

The man absorbed her words and his eyes widened. "I saw a butterfly, too. And a great whale." Struggling with some internal demon, he tried to rise but gave up before managing the task.

"Can I help?" Juan Pablo started to drop his bags.

"My only help comes in a bottle." He looked at his half-full bottle and set it aside. He struggled again to rise. He came to his feet and stood for several seconds, teetering unsteadily.

The demon won and he sat back down.

It occurred to Juan Pablo to ask: "Where did you see this butterfly and whale?"

"Here." The man pointed between his two eyes. "Right here."

Rocio looked at him. In the way of close friends, he knew what she was thinking. That the man was loco. Maybe, but Juan Pablo remembered his abuela's sight came that way too. Uncertain like the wind, and sometimes the funniest echo of a real thing. Once her sight showed her a giant lizard and she agonized over what it meant, until later that day their neighbors invited them to watch a Godzilla movie on TV. Another time she saw a hole swallowing up Juan Pablo's legs. She worried that an accident might somehow cause him to lose his legs. He fell all right, but only tore two giant holes in his jeans. Another time she saw herself being pulled into the earth by her long braid and two days later, when helping a new mom with her newborn, her braid got pulled into a vacuum. The sight was never reasonable, she always said. Not really good for much but scaring an old woman.

"I have always dreamed of seeing a whale," Rocio said, and indeed she spoke in a dreamy voice. "Not on TV or in a museum. A real one," she added, her voice changing with hope.

"Me too," Juan Pablo said.

The old man's smile was an unused instrument.

His abuela used to say, *Some smiles are a gift from above.*

"I need coffee," he said. "And enough food to last the both of you two days at least, but just juice and fruit for me."

Juan Pablo could scarcely believe their luck. "You'll take us?"

"You have to buy the petro."

"How much?"

He stated a number. Rocio gasped. The old man misunderstood, and looking out over the big blue, he explained, "The winds are good. The sea is calm. We can probably sail most of the way, but just in case, we have to have petro."

"Sí, señor. We will buy all the petro you need. Gracias, gracias."

Rocio and Juan Pablo leapt into action, turning and rushing off to the small store.

As Rocio shopped for their food, Juan Pablo got a cup of coffee.

The store clerk, heavyset and friendly, asked, "Is this for the padre?"

"Padre?"

She motioned outside to the *Catori*. "The old man."

"Sí," Juan Pablo said. "Is he a padre?"

She nodded. "He used to be the most loved padre. Before."

"Before?"

"Before"—she sighed, shaking her head—"all the trouble." She said noncommittally, "No charge for the padre," and waved him away.

Juan Pablo returned to the boat with coffee but found the old man fast asleep again. He woke him gently, just like before, but this time he held the treasure of a strong cup of black coffee.

The man accepted the offering, and Juan Pablo turned to leave. He stopped suddenly, as a thought broke through his excitement. "Padre, do you think we will see a whale?"

The old man nodded. "The grays are migrating now. The mysticetes sometimes grace us with a sighting."

Juan Pablo could not hide his excitement. "Gracias, Padre," he yelled before running off to help Rocio.

He found Rocio at the market and told her the old man was a padre.

Rocio's eyebrows rose. "He does not look like a padre."

"There was trouble."

Rocio froze with alarm. "What kind of trouble?"

Juan Pablo shrugged. He knew it mattered, but he didn't want to worry Rocio more. "He's probably retired now."

She searched his face, seeking reassurance. "The butterfly . . ."

Juan Pablo nodded. "We will be safe with him."

Rocio nodded before returning to the task at hand. She found the peanut butter and dropped it in the basket. He thought to distract her and related the important news about the whales.

"That's right. They are migrating now. I will have my phone ready. I still have half a charge. I won't use it till we see our whale."

"To see a whale. Just to be on a boat. I have never been on a boat," Juan Pablo realized.

"Me either. The best part is—"

Juan Pablo finished for her: "No one can find us on a small boat in the middle of the ocean." This was the best part. The man with the red boots could not reach them on a boat. The idea of being safe, really safe, if just for the space of the crossing, made Juan Pablo urge, "Hurry, Rocio."

Within the next hour, the padre had tightly packed the groceries in the tiny cabinets: granola, cheese, peanut butter, tortillas, and almond milk for them and apples and orange juice for the old man. He showed them how to prepare for launch, and for nearly an hour, the two busied themselves with this work.

Finally, the small boat headed beneath the midday sun on a cloudless day into the big blue. The darker blue sea mirrored the lighter bowl of blue sky. Gulls followed their path out to sea, squawking with their same excitement and sometimes flying so close they could touch them. He and Rocio sat in the stern, watching Mazatlán push away until even the lighthouse disappeared into the blue horizon, taking their fears with it. It felt like an auspicious beginning.

Smiles grew into laughter; he and Rocio soon discovered they loved sailing.

By afternoon the *Catori* had passed thirteen fishing boats and been passed by eight other sailboats and two ferries. The wind slapped the sails and the sea lapped at the sides of their small vessel. Their wake rolled back into the sea, disappearing behind them into the glassy surface.

Rocio stood at the stern, binoculars in hand, searching the horizon for whales. Juan Pablo sat starboard, arms folded over his knees and transfixed, he contented himself with staring out. His abuela, too, always wanted to see a whale, which was one of three sacred species, joining elephants and, of course, the butterflies.

These are special souls from the spiritual realm.

How do you know this? He always asked this question, because his abuela's answers were so interesting.

You can tell because almost all people have a wealth of heart energy for them; people everywhere want to see them, touch them, draw close to their presence. Their spiritual purpose is to use this heart energy to connect people to the plight of all living things on earth.

The sunlight sparkled over the surface of the vast blue space.

As he stared out, he began to notice that when he thought of his abuela, the sparkling sun on the water began to dance merrily across the ocean surface. The more he thought of her, the faster the sparkles seemed to dance. As if saying out loud, *I am still here, Juan Pablo, just different.* If he thought of anything else, like his violin or Rocio, the sparkling light quieted.

Was his abuela making the sunlight dance for him so he would know she was still with him? Or was it just his imagination?

"Rocio, I want you to see something. Sit here for a moment."

Smiling, Rocio sat next to him expectantly.

"See the sunlight sparkling on the water?"

She nodded. "It is beautiful. Like a thousand diamonds set upon the water."

"Now think of your abuelo. Think of how much he loves you."

"That is easy to do."

"Does the light change when you think of his love?"

For a long moment she stared out over the water, her face changing with the awareness. "JP, the sparkles. They start moving fast and faster still. Like they are . . ."

"Dancing." Juan Pablo laughed. "It is a trick of our imagination."

"Or maybe a miracle."

After showing them how to help sail the boat, the padre spoke little. When he wasn't attending to the boat, he read from a worn book titled *Vida y doctrinas de Jesús* by Thomas Jefferson, the third American president. He fell asleep in the afternoon—or Juan Pablo thought he was sleeping, until he heard an unexpected request.

"Son, are you any good on that instrument?"

Juan Pablo shrugged, pretending modesty as his abuela had taught him to do.

"Play an old man a piece, will you?"

Rocio smiled at him encouragingly. He would love nothing more. To keep his violin safe and dry, the old man had placed his precious case atop old snorkeling masks and fins, a rope, a couple of life jackets, and assorted fishing gear in a storage bin. Juan Pablo retrieved it and thinking of his abuela, he began with her favorite piece, *Esta Tarde Vi Llover.*

Within minutes, he was lost to everything but the music.

Juan Pablo did not see the old man's surprise as he measured the manifestation of talent and laid it alongside the young man's age. He had the padre's full attention. The old man moved closer to the sound, drawn like most people to the impossibly haunting sounds rising from Juan Pablo's instrument.

The old man listened with his head down, not wanting to share the pleasure with his other senses. He removed his hat to wipe at something in his eye.

When he finished with that piece, Rocio said, "JP, play the one you played for the rich American at her daughter's wedding."

Juan Pablo played the familiar piece and ended with "Here Comes the Bride," which made Rocio laugh.

"My god," the old man said softly. "If you were full grown, you'd be a talented musician. That you are so young . . ." He shook his head. "Music is God's gift to man, to make life bearable. It is the only art of heaven given to earth, the only art of earth that we take to heaven."

This familiar quote delighted Juan Pablo. "My abuela always said that!"

The old man's eyes suddenly went soft. "Your abuela died recently."

Juan Pablo nodded. "And Rocio's abuelo on the same day."

Rocio fingered a small hole in the deck suddenly.

"What happened?"

Rocio looked up at Juan Pablo.

The story came out in bits and pieces. He would start and Rocio would finish or vice versa. The scary parts were dispensed in a breathless hurry: the gruesome deaths, the phones going off in close succession, his abuela leaving the world, followed by Rocio's abuelo's heart attack, the man following them with the red boots, and the disappearance of Rocio's uncle.

Just the retelling caused their hearts to race.

By the end, Rocio and Juan Pablo were holding each other's hands.

The padre swore under his breath. "Goddamn drugs—the devil's tool. Making beasts of all of us." He removed his cap, rubbed his forehead, and replaced it, a gesture somehow nervous, as if bracing for pain. "So, how will we escape this red-booted monster?"

Juan Pablo opened the case to return his violin. He told him of his abuela's strange last words.

"Who will be waiting for you?"

Juan Pablo shook his head. He still did not altogether believe in miracles, but so far, the butterflies had not led them wrong. He trusted no one more than his abuela and because of this, he knew that if no one was waiting for him in Pacific Grove, it wouldn't matter. He still had to make the journey.

"Somehow we must get to America."

"Your abuela will see you to California," the old man told Juan Pablo, as if it were not just a hope. "The hard part is getting the girl to Arizona. But . . . I might be able to help."

Rocio studied the old man before asking softly, "But how can you help? Will the *Catori* take us up Baja's coast?"

"If only she could. She could never weather the open Pacific. Ah," he sighed, "she is too old now."

"Then . . . how?"

"Let us see what happens when we reach Cabo," he said noncommittally.

Rocio's gaze shot to Juan Pablo. He shrugged. Maybe the old man could help. After all, a butterfly led them to the padre.

"Are you really a padre?" Juan Pablo asked.

"Not anymore."

"Because of . . . the trouble?"

"The *trouble*. My troubles, your troubles. The same trouble that plagues us all." The old man turned his sad, weathered face to the sea. "It's rising up from the depth of hell . . ."

Rocio and JP exchanged confused looks, but the padre said no more.

Sometime later the boat suddenly stopped. They looked over and saw the old man staring through binoculars at something in the distance. Their gazes followed. A bright red and blue sheet of something floated in the water.

"What is it?" Juan Pablo asked.

The wind and the water drowned out the old man's voice, but they thought he said "trash." He expertly maneuvered the sails. It took a quarter of an hour, but at last they pulled alongside. Juan Pablo and Rocio stared at a clump of floating rubbish piled up on a large piece of red and blue canvas, the colors all but faded in the elements.

The old man began hauling the mess onboard with Rocio and Juan Pablo's help. A lot of Styrofoam, a buoy, tangled fishing nets, three giant plastic water bottles, countless smaller bottles of water, two children's toys, all floating together in a mini island of trash.

"Oh, a diaper," Rocio gave a start, dropping it back. The old man fished it out again. The ocean had eroded it all to the bare essence. Once everything was onboard, he shoved it into a corner and returned to right the sails.

The *Catori* aimed straight for the setting sun.

The air grew chilly and they donned sweatshirts and ate tortillas and peanut butter while Padre poured another cup of orange juice. The old man gave them two worn, cracked deck cushions and two blankets and they set up camp on the deck.

Stars came up one by one until they littered the night sky.

Juan Pablo sat staring out to sea. The wind and water were quieter in the darkness and more mysterious because of the unseen depths.

Juan Pablo gathered his courage. "Padre, was your trouble like ours?"

He grimaced, nodding. "It is the trouble swallowing up our whole beautiful country . . ."

The story came out slowly in a voice weighted by sadness and set against the backdrop of the steady breeze and the boat plowing through the sea. He and Rocio lay side by side, staring up into the velvet night sky as they listened.

The cartel moved into the padre's parish in Monterrey. At first few people noticed. "The Americans have a saying, like frogs in a frying pan. It is a good saying, because change comes so gradually at first and you don't realize how much trouble you are in until it is too late . . ." Extortion fees rose; businesses began closing. At first a few people went "missing," but where did they go? Did they move out? No one seemed to know for sure. Then there were rumors of dark deeds. The one that got the most attention were the missing dogs. Within two years, the police became useless; those that weren't on the take were killed or forced out.

The padre kept going to his superiors for help, but, "Each time I saw my own fear staring back at me." He was told to pray, but "Prayer became little more than a succor of the helpless. Every day another story, another tragedy. I had to do something, I had to . . ."

The padre finally stumbled on a means to combat the growing scourge. He started drug rehabilitation centers. At least he could help some of the people separate themselves from this evil and return them to life. His success emboldened him; he felt he was being guided by heaven. First one, then three more. He began organizing his parishioners to demand the government begin cleaning up the police departments.

The old man shook his head and fell silent for a long minute, remembering. "More and more people came for help every day. The church started to pay attention. People began volunteering and raising some good money. Hundreds, maybe thousands of people were finally getting the help they needed."

The padre's voice drifted off again, as if it was the end of the story, but that would have been a happy story and Juan Pablo and Rocio knew from his tone that this was not that.

"What happened then?" Juan Pablo asked.

"Just as goodness multiplies, so too the opposite. Which is the stronger force? I always thought I knew the answer. The cartels blew up two of the clinics. They killed five people in the first one and two in the second. Within a day, the third one was empty. I was first devastated, but then angry. I wanted to rebuild, but there was no money. Worse, fear began spreading again. Once again we became victims.

"Humans," he said in an altered voice. "Our rapacious greed. It consumes everything—a monster unleashed on the world."

The sounds of the sea returned in their shared silence.

Rocio felt for Juan Pablo's hand again.

"We will be safe in America," Rocio whispered.

"Sí," Juan Pablo said.

"America," the padre muttered under his breath, shaking his head. "The money comes from that golden place, you know. Billions upon billions of dollars. Besides, the cartels do not respect the border; their tentacles are reaching ever further el norte."

Juan Pablo didn't believe this; he couldn't believe this. America was still safe. The police were honest; the laws were respected in most parts of the United States. People went about their lives, normal, good lives, untouched by this violence. It was still the shining place where dreams came true . . .

"JP, look."

A full moon rose over the sea.

The rising moon became a lantern over their shared dreams, whispered between themselves. Juan Pablo spun a happy tale for

Rocio, presenting her with their best-case scenario: Rocio would go to school in America; everyone would be impressed by how well she spoke and read both English and Spanish, by how advanced she was in math. She would shine like one of the very stars above them.

"Which star?" Rocio asked.

"That one," he pointed. "The brightest one."

"And you, JP. You will finally go to a music school, the best one and finally, finally, you will discover the sad truth."

"What truth is that?" Juan Pablo asked.

"That you are not the very best, most accomplished musician in the world."

Juan Pablo asked through his laughter, "But how can that happen?"

Rocio hit him playfully on his arm.

For a moment they fell silent, bathed in the magic spell cast by a full moon. A shimmering trail of it went from their boat back up to the moon. "It looks like a path to heaven," Rocio whispered. "This is what the whales see every night. The light reaching back up to the stars."

"They must wonder about the moon and the stars just like us," Juan Pablo said. "Remember when I found the recording of the whale song and I played it and Tajo sat up and listened with his head cocked? It was as if he understood something we could not."

Rocio squeezed his hand but said nothing. The loss of Tajo was still a raw wound. She had so loved the little guy. Someday he would surprise her with a puppy.

Until that happy moment, he thought to distract her. "Remember we watched the Discovery Channel video of the migrating whales?"

"Sí," Rocio said. "From Alaska in America all the way down to Mexico. Their babies are born here in the warm waters of the Sea of Cortez."

"Remember how they kept close to the shore to avoid the orcas? How the orcas sometimes eat the baby gray whales?"

"Sí. It was so sad."

The documentary emphasized that this was still not the whales' greatest threat, that what truly threatened them was that the oceans were changing, that humans were changing it. Maybe it was true, that human's rapacious greed was consuming everything—indeed, as the padre said, this greed was a monster unleashed on the world.

Rocio's sadness reached into him. He thought of all they had lost at the hands of this monster: his abuela, their home, and maybe even the whales and the butterflies. "Everywhere we turn there is sadness."

"And still it is so beautiful," Rocio whispered, answering him.

CHAPTER ELEVEN

Dawn spread over the darkness. Juan Pablo stirred in his sleep. He first heard a distant sound, a sad cry of distress and hopelessness. It struck his heart and he knew fear. He tried to find the source but saw only deep darkness. His abuela appeared and his heart leapt to greet this happy sight, but she was not happy.

Wake up now, Juan Pablo.

He came full awake. The sails flapped gently in a mild breeze. Padre snored loudly. The sun rose in the east and the sea looked dark and deep, and as smooth as a mirror. He sat up to take stock of the new day. Then he saw it.

"Wake up, Rocio. Look!"

Land in the distance. Baja California. They would be docking this very afternoon.

"This is our big chance," Rocio said, jumping up. "I need the binoculars."

Juan Pablo stood up and stared out at the distant roll of brown hills.

Several minutes passed before Rocio directed him to a ripple in the water. "What is that?"

They studied the wake for several more minutes before their joined gasps sounded in the still air. About a hundred meters away, the whale sliced through the water. "JP," Rocio whispered urgently, as if a loud voice might scare it away. It was too huge to be seen all at once. First the massive arch of a barnacled back emerged followed by its dorsal fin, and finally a fifteen-foot tail shot out of the water. The tail seemed to hover for a few seconds, as if waving goodbye before slipping below.

Juan Pablo gave a huge shout.

Rocio's breath caught in her throat, and her eyes grew wide as if to encompass an enormity that surpassed her wildest expectations.

Juan Pablo was jumping up and down like a kid. "I saw a whale. I saw a whale."

"Wait." Rocio grabbed his arm, noticing something in the water about fifty meters from the boat. A lump of dark gray poked from the water. "What's that out there? A rock?" She looked in its direction.

"I don't know," Juan Pablo said.

A spout emerged from the rock. Juan Pablo gasped.

"Rocio . . ."

With her long hair lifted into a bun, held by a plastic fork, and tendrils circling around her like a halo, Rocio stood at the bow, binoculars to eyes as she studied the spot.

"It is not moving. Is it . . . is it dead?"

"A spout!"

Nearby, a second spout shot straight in the air. The giant tail slipped smoothly into the calm water.

The children jumped with excitement, sending a loud and long cheer into the air.

But the closer one barely moved.

Roused by the noise, Padre came to stand beside them. He took the binoculars from Rocio and aimed them at the whales for a long moment. "It's a baby, but something is wrong."

He rushed to the sails and slowly aimed the boat in toward them.

The words cautioned them and their excitement disappeared in the instant.

"Something's wrong?" They braced for terrible news.

Rocio and Juan Pablo stared, barely breathing as they watched the giant baby whale come closer into view. Smooth and gray and much too still. Bright yellow rope wrapped dozens of times all around it. The old man rushed to the side, staring at it.

"¡Santo cielos!" He expelled the words. "She's tangled in fishing net."

The old man flew into action, moving swiftly, as if he had done this a hundred times. He lifted the seat cupboard and reached in, withdrawing a mask. Holding this, he took off his shirt and pants, and slipped out of his flip-flops before diving into the blue depth.

He emerged twenty paces from the boat. He shook his head and expertly fitted his mask over his face. Face-down in the water, he swam to the baby whale.

Rocio and Juan Pablo leaned far over the rail to see.

The mother whale suddenly spouted very close. Rocio and Juan Pablo gasped in unison as a fifteen-foot spray shot into the stilled air. A good-sized wave rocked the boat from the whale's breach.

The old man swam in a tight circle around the baby whale. Emerging, he called back to them. "Get me my knife. It's in the cabinet above the steerage."

Juan Pablo raced into action. He found the knife, about ten inches long, and ran back to the boat's stern. Before Padre could stop him, he discarded his sweater, the T-shirt beneath, and his jeans. Clutching the knife tightly, he jumped in.

The cold water enveloped him. He came up for air, and still tightly clutching the knife, he swam slowly toward the baby whale. Padre was shouting at him, but he couldn't hear the words above the racing of his heart.

A massive dark shape, much bigger than the boat, swam slowly under Juan Pablo. He held his breath and froze as the displaced water first lifted him up and then pulled him down. He emerged a minute later, took a gulp of breath, and looked around. The old man was nowhere to be seen. He heard Rocio scream something from the boat. "Captain!"

The old man popped up, took a breath, and submerged again. Juan Pablo swam toward him. All at once he understood what was happening. The mother whale swam under the baby, lifting her up to get air. A small spout erupted just as the old man appeared at his side.

He shouted, "The knife, JP, the knife."

Juan Pablo passed it to the old man. Knife in hand he disappeared again. Juan Pablo tread water, watching. He made out the padre's puny form near the baby whale. The baby held still as the padre cut the fishing net. Juan Pablo moved closer. The fishing net was wrapped many times around the baby's fins and tail, as if it had rolled over and over, maybe to escape the terrible trap, but instead tangling itself worse.

Rocio called something from the boat. He looked over to see the girl waving frantically. He looked down again and saw. The mother whale swam slowly back and forth beneath her baby, turned slightly to look, moving very slow.

The padre emerged again and in between gasps, he managed, "It looks bad for her. She's weak and so tangled. We're going to need more help."

Juan Pablo felt the man's desperation across the short distance. "I can help. I can hold my breath for two minutes and thirty-eight seconds."

The padre paused for just a moment.

He repeated, "I can help!"

"Go back to the boat, boy. There's scissors in the same place and another mask. Be sure to fit it before you swim out."

Juan Pablo swam fast and furious back to the boat. He told Rocio. The girl ran off, returning moments later with the scissors. She bent over and handed these to Juan Pablo. She found a mask. "Make it tight," Juan Pablo called up. The girl fumbled with the mask for several seconds before handing this down to him.

Juan Pablo soon realized he couldn't get the mask on while holding the scissors. He reached them back up to Rocio. He fixed the mask on his face. Once he had the scissors in hand, he was off.

Face-down, the scene appeared in frightening clarity. The mother whale swam maybe thirty meters beneath them. She appeared as a slow-moving dark shadow, dotted with crusty barnacles, like speckled dots along the whole of her. She was huge, twice as long as the *Catori*. He felt her heightened interest, but perhaps he only imagined this as he swam to her baby.

No, it was not his imagination. A deep slow echo pushed through the water, the most forlorn cry for help.

I will help, he thought. *I will help or die trying . . .*

Heart pounding with the emergency, he took in the sight. The old man braced one hand on the baby as he deftly cut the net around the body. She was maybe three meters wide and fifteen to twenty meters long, a miniature of her mother. The padre had almost freed one dorsal fin before he emerged for air. Juan Pablo emerged alongside the old man, a meter away from the calf.

"Be very careful," he managed between gasps for breath. "She can take you down with a roll. You hear? Keep at arm's distance, or as far away as you can while cutting the rope."

Juan Pablo nodded and taking a big gulp, he disappeared at her tail. His first touch sent a thrill through him—the smoothest, slippery surface—but he didn't have time to think, only act. Holding the scissors, he snapped once, then again and one more time before he pushed himself up for air.

He came up with a huge gasp. The mother whale moved directly below. He realized what was happening. Padre saw it, too. They pushed hard backward as the mother whale rose beneath her baby, lifting her up for a breath.

The spout, the sign of life, fell over Juan Pablo's head.

Stripped to her underwear, Rocio dove in. She came up and fitted a pair of goggles over her eyes before swimming to Juan Pablo's side. "I don't have a knife, but I can pull the rope away from her and you cut."

Juan Pablo nodded.

As soon as the mother disappeared below, they swam to her baby. Rocio spent a full minute studying the whale before coming up for air. She dipped down again, pointing to a spot. He took a big gulp, and dove. Right off he saw the smart strategy of cutting where she pointed. She lifted the rope away as he cut. With Rocio's help, he was able to cut again and again, while his other hand pulled the loosened net from her tail.

Rocio's long hair floated around her face. She had to be careful not to get it tangled in the net as they repeated the measure dozens of times. The padre did the same, freeing the first dorsal fin. Grabbing a precious breath, the old man swam around the baby and emerged on her other side.

He cut and cut and pulled with all his strength.

As they worked, the mother emerged like clockwork to lift her baby up, six, seven, eight times.

Juan Pablo ignored the cold seeping into his bones. He ignored his now cut and bleeding fingers, the sting of salt water. He ignored his thirst for air. He thought only of the *snap, snap, snap* of the scissors on the deadly fishing net.

The baby whale seemed to have tremors now, like tiny earthquakes running the length of her.

Juan Pablo and Rocio emerged to find the old man waiting for them.

"One more . . . cut . . . fins will be free." He tried to steady his breath.

Juan Pablo nodded, his heart pounding furiously as he tread water. Rocio nodded too, but the old man's gasps reminded her of her abuelo. "Are you okay, Padre?"

"I can't—" Gasps for air. "I can't cut it—tail must be free. First. We have to do the last cuts at the same time. She's ready to go—how much more?"

"Three more cuts, I think."

"Okay. Move."

They took a deep breath and descended two feet. They released their breath in bubbles. Rocio held the rope up as Juan Pablo cut three times before he pulled with all his might. The old man freed the dorsal fin. As Juan Pablo and Rocio held the net, the baby whale shimmied forward. They held the net with all of their strength. Juan Pablo closed his eyes, his heart urging the baby forward with a silent explosion of joy.

The net came free. He and Rocio popped up. Padre emerged as well.

The old man gave a big shout. Juan Pablo yelled, just as he and Rocio began laughing triumphantly, their joy a tangible force.

The baby gave a tentative go of swimming. The mother rose a short distance below her.

"Watch out," the old man warned them.

Juan Pablo and Rocio tread water, witnessing it.

The morning sun caught the spout and a rainbow arced over them.

Joined by tears and laughter, the three wet people stood on the deck of the *Catori* watching a fine show made from a mother's gratitude. As the whales swam away, the mother's ten-meter tail shot out of the water and hovered a few seconds before slipping back down below.

Juan Pablo and Rocio collapsed on the deck on their hands and knees.

Rocio threw her arms around him and he held her cold, wet form against himself as they tried to calm their still-racing hearts. Full of joy and triumph, they laughed. If he had one wish it would be that his abuela really was watching from a lofty plane, that she had witnessed this great thing Rocio and her grandson had done.

The morning light danced and sparkled merrily over the tiny ripples in the sea . . .

CHAPTER TWELVE

The padre could hardly tear his gaze from the raised dais in the packed barroom where the teenager played Vivaldi's Concerto in D Minor. The boisterous crowd had fallen silent too, mesmerized by the performance. The room exploded with applause as Juan Pablo took his last bow, his face beaming with pride. His abuela would have tsk-tsked him, but she would have been smiling, too.

People crowded around his violin case, filling it with pesos and dollars. Compliments flew at Juan Pablo. Shaking hands, saying "Gracias" over and over, he made his way through the smoke-filled room to the padre sitting at the bar.

If only Rocio was here to witness this. He still couldn't believe she was gone.

It all happened so fast. Once the *Catori* had reached Cabo San Lucas's harbor and the picturesque city of hotels, condominiums, and restaurants set before the sun-bleached cliffs, the old man had refused, absolutely, to hear of them leaving. He explained the reality to them: There was no way a beautiful young girl could cross the border without protection, let alone if they were being hunted by the cursed cartel. They wouldn't make it out of the city. He might have a trick he could pull off; he knew someone, a rich and powerful person, and he was owed a favor. They were to wait for his return

He and Rocio had spent three days magical days of swimming in the ocean, walking the streets, and picnicking in the park every night. They had no idea where the padre had gone until he had returned in the middle of the third night bearing the miraculous gift: A passport and an American birth certificate for Rocio.

How he and Rocio had clung to each other at the airport.

Juan Pablo finally reached the padre's side.

The old man patted his back affectionately. "Ah, the maestro!"

Flushed and happy, Juan Pablo gratefully accepted the icy water the bartender set before him. Still, all he could think about was Rocio. He closed his eyes, the sweet scent of her freshly washed hair coming back to him. He recited her last text from memory: *Everything is so shiny in America. The plane flight was just like in the movies, but without the snakes. My mom's here!*

He and the padre had come to the bar to celebrate.

An older man was pushing his way through the crowded bar toward them.

Noticing his friend, the padre smiled. "Dario." Holding his drink as if offering a toast to Juan Pablo, he shouted to be heard, "Did you hear my young friend play? The music comes straight from heaven, no?"

"Sí, sí." The man stood between the padre and Juan Pablo, facing the bar. He was clearly a working man: white T-shirt, worn Levi's, and work boots. "You are a very talented young man."

Juan Pablo started to smile, but the worry in the man's eyes alerted him. Dario was searching the mirror behind them over the bar, anxiously examining the faces that surrounded them.

Fear pushed through Juan Pablo's body; he knew what he was going to say before he said it.

"That is why I am telling you this," he said, head bent forward, so as not to be overheard. "People are looking for you." His gaze motioned to Juan Pablo. "The wrong kind of people."

The padre slowly set down his drink. "Who?"

"You know, Hector over on the avenue?"

The padre did know of the man. "Droguista."

"He is showing a picture on his phone. Juan Pablo's location, he says, is worth two thousand."

"Pesos?" Juan Pablo asked.

Dario shook his head. "Not pesos."

A tingling alarm shot through Juan Pablo. His picture plastered over the Internet, the great World Wide Web that covered the entire earth, just as that old Indian predicted a hundred years ago: *The land shall be crisscrossed by a giant spider's web.* Everyone would be looking for him—everyone who needed money, which was basically, 7-plus billion people.

"When?" the padre asked.

"About an hour ago," he answered, running his callused hands nervously through his long gray hair. "He is asking everyone. I came straight over."

Looking nervously around the room, Juan Pablo swallowed his panic. The man with the red boots was not going to give up. The cartel was not going to give up. His fate was sealed; he was a doomed creature, like a pig at slaughter, the end was upon him . . .

The padre tossed a couple of pesos on the bar. "Get your violin," he ordered in a heated whisper as he stood up to leave.

Dazed, afraid to look at anyone now, Juan Pablo made his way across the room to his violin. He quickly packed up, managing to nod and smile at the well-wishers as he followed the padre out the door.

Once outside, a warm breeze from the sea greeted them, but it did nothing to ease their fear. The harbor, marked by dozens of lights, stretched before them. A large cruise ship had just docked that morning and hundreds of tourists mixed with the locals on the main boulevard. Burdened by his violin, dodging people as he went, Juan Pablo raced to keep up with the padre. The old man was a good ten meters ahead, drunkenly cursing under his breath, which Juan Pablo had noticed happened whenever he drank. People parted to get out of the madman's way. They passed the American Hard Rock Cafe, the padre rushing forward to get back to their slip and the relative safety of the *Catori*.

Finally catching up, Juan Pablo listened with little understanding of the man's drunken, muttered words as they hurried down the street.

"Why did you shackle me with this useless heart? What good is it? This fucking albatross beating its wings against my chest, dooming me all my days." He lost sight of the old man behind a costumed mariachi band strolling through the crowds as they played. He ran to reach his side again. For an old man, he could be quick. "I don't even need to hear the entreaties of their angels; I know they're special . . ."

"I do not want you to get in trouble, Padre. If you were to get hurt hiding me—"

Upon hearing this, the padre stopped as if quite shocked. Glancing in both directions, he spotted an alleyway between a hotel and another bar. He grabbed Juan Pablo's arm and pulled him into the shadows there. "Juan Pablo, I will not let them have you. Do you understand?" A fierce passion fueled his gaze. "I have lost everything. So many have lost everything."

"But—"

"No." The padre cut him off. "They are not going to get you, too, so help me God."

The old man resumed walking again, heading down the dock for the boat.

Juan Pablo ran after him. "But . . . but we cannot hide forever, and you said the *Catori* cannot make it up the Baja coast."

The padre stepped onboard the darkened boat. "We don't need to hide forever. Only for two days." Then, aiming the words toward the heavens, "Two days, that's all I ask."

Juan Pablo climbed onboard after him. "Then what will we do?" He stored his violin and his backpack, hurrying to help man the ship.

"Not we, but you, Juan Pablo. You see, I booked you on an American cruise ship going to San Diego . . ."

CHAPTER THIRTEEN

Juan Pablo woke to a furious pounding.

"Hey, hey, kid. Time to wake up."

Darkness surrounded him. He was enclosed, knees to chest in a small, tight, dark space. His backpack rested on his knees and his violin case stood at his side, pointing up.

The latch lifted up and an overhead light shined bright. A face appeared. "Hurry up, kid."

The voice sounded American.

A light shone from behind an attractive face. Reddish hair, cut short and slicked back with grease. Amber eyes and an angular face made of sharp lines, the man might have been handsome, except for the pointy chin.

"Rise and shine kid. The cones are about to pop."

"Cones? Pop?"

"Passengers, kid. The passengers are about to start waking up and I need you topside before a shirt comes by."

Juan Pablo tried to stand up. "Kenny Backdoor?" He had met the man last night, but it had been dark. He and the padre took a long time to say their goodbyes; only in parting did he realize he had come to love the old man. The padre did not have a phone, so he was instructed to call a church in Monterrey when he was safe. The priest there would get word back to him.

The magician's cart was hauled onboard the giant cruise ship. He had thought he'd get out right away, but no one came for hours. He must have eventually fallen asleep.

"That's Backdoor Kenny. You can call me BK. Here, let me help you out. We've really got to get moving."

Juan Pablo lifted his backpack and violin before trying to climb out. His legs hurt from the cramped position, and standing was a sweet relief. He leapt out.

"Hey. You're one tall kid. A myuzo, too, huh?"

"Myuzo?"

"The violin. A musician?"

Juan Pablo nodded as he took in the strange surroundings. A bright light shone over the pale blue linoleum floor and pink walls of the small cabin, roughly a quarter of the size of his bedroom in El Rosario. A bunk, a tiny desk, a closet, that was all. The cart he just climbed out of took up most of the available space.

"Okay, now listen up, kid. The old man gave me two grand to see you to San Diego and in order to do this—"

"The padre gave you two grand—two thousand pesos?"

"Huh!" BK expelled his breath in a dismissive gust. "Pesos? Geezus. No. Good ol' greenbacks, kid. Which I was more than happy to take because one, I hate this fucking job and if we get caught I won't mind all that much getting fired, and two, I owed the old man a favor, a big favor and this is it. Now—"

"But . . . but how did he pay you? The padre has no money."

"A big wad of cash, kid."

"But . . . but where did he get the money?"

"Sold his boat. To some schmuck who imagines Americans will be clamoring to climb aboard that floating piece of driftwood to get a two-minute look at some whale."

Juan Pablo's eyes widened. The padre sold his beloved *Catori* to get him to safety. "He never said . . . he . . . but, what will he do without the *Catori*?"

"Ah, that. He's going to put the collar back on, kid. Head back to the war zone. Some do-gooder shit for all the kids like you. You were just his first, I guess."

"But—"

BK cut him off. "I don't know any more. I wasn't really paying attention after he handed over the cash."

BK misunderstood Juan Pablo's stricken look. "Hey, hey. I'm good for it. I owe the man my life, for what little that's worth." He chuckled. "About two grand, I guess. That is provided I can, let's just say, keep my fucking hands clean. Okay"—he rubbed his hands together—"first rule: Find me in the casino after midnight. I'll take you back in the cart. You sleep there." He pointed under the bunk. "Stow your things here." He pointed to the closet. "You have free run of the ship, but for God's sake, keep a low profile. Do not attract attention from a shirt."

"Shirt?" Juan Pablo looked at his butterfly T-shirt.

"Officers. Anyone wearing a uniform. If anyone asks, and they won't—we're all so dark here, bone tired, stressed, overworked—people can't see past their damn nose. Just say you're in cabin 2014."

"Cabin 2014," Juan Pablo repeated.

"And if anyone asks, and again, they won't, just say your mom is sleeping. Got it?"

Juan Pablo nodded.

BK sized him up. "You kind of look American, the height and those odd green eyes, so that's good. How's your English? The old man said you speak it very well."

"I try to speak English as much as possible. Rocio and I only speak English to each other—"

"Still got an accent, but never mind. Just don't get all chatty with any adults, okay? Kids don't give a shit where you're from, do they? What do you like to do? You like to swim? Got some trunks in there?"

Juan Pablo looked to his backpack. He did not have any swim trunks. "I love to swim, but I use my underwear."

"Not cool here." He went to a drawer and pulled out a pair of black and red swim trunks. "Try this. You should probably put them

141

on now. Do you have flip-flops in there? Those sneakers look ready to fall off. You got to look like part of the tribe."

"I don't have any sandals, if that's what you mean," Juan Pablo said as he began removing his jeans. These were carefully folded and placed in his backpack. He slipped on the trunks, only to find they were several sizes too big. He tightened the string.

"Good enough," BK said. "Okay, okay. You have any money?"

Juan Pablo nodded. "A little."

"There's a store onboard. Buy some flip-flops. Ditch the sneakers when you can. Take everything you need for the day, because you can't come back until after midnight."

Juan Pablo gathered his money and his iPad, placing them in his abuela's shopping bag.

"You look kind of cool," BK said, seeing the bright blue bag with a large orange butterfly on it. "Maybe a little ah, eccentric, but hey, every myuzo I know is that. Okay, let's go. I'll cart you topside and then, the ship is yours, kid."

With a sigh, Juan Pablo climbed back in and soon BK was pushing the cart down the I-95, the main corridor below deck and the most crowded space on the floating city.

Dear Rocio:
You will never guess where I am.

But first write back right away and tell me if there is any news about your uncle. I keep thinking of him, hoping he is okay. What does your mom say? Did you tell her everything?

Now, for my news. I am on a cruise ship. Sí. I feel like I am in a dream. I am sitting in a large and fine room on a ship. It is like a floating city for rich people. Yesterday I spent all day wandering the decks and swimming. There are eight decks, if you don't count the two below. Guess what? It has two swimming pools, one with waves! Because no one notices me, I got up my courage and went in a Jacuzzi. You've seen them in movies. Small, hot pools of water. It felt so good! They are everywhere! Best of all, free food. All-you-can-eat ice cream, pizza, and sodas. Six restaurants in all, but the main dining hall is buffet-style with all-you-can-eat breakfast, lunch, and dinner.

The padre arranged the whole thing. He paid a man named BK who works on the ship as a bartender, a magician, and a card dealer. He snuck me onboard in his magician's cart. I sleep in his cabin, under his bunk. BK snores, but I don't mind.

I will be in San Diego, California, in three days.

After BK finishes at the casino, I get back in his cart and he returns me to his cabin. Last night he let me look out as we returned to the lower deck, because no one was around. All the workers live below the decks. It is like a poorer city down there. BK says the crew just pretends to be happy for the people above, but that working on the ship is slave labor: long hours and low pay. Sometimes no pay because the workers have to pay back the people who got them the job and it takes forever.

Not like the passengers. The passengers live like kings.

The best part is I get to go topside during the day. I pretend I am someone's kid, but BK said no one will bother asking me who I am and he was right. No one notices me. Yesterday I swam all day in the pool. Afterward I saw two movies in the theater and then I got to watch BK's magic show, which was interesting. I don't know how he does some of the tricks, and he won't tell me. He says why spoil the magic? He says it is his secret, but he said only a fool would allow a magician at the card tables.

I am safe, like you Rocio. The ship is in Mexican waters, sí, but it is an American ship and the man with the red boots is far, far away now. Soon I will be in San Diego, America. I will take the

*train or a bus to Pacific Grove, CA. Then, when I see who is there,
if anyone is there for me, I will come to Arizona and visit you.*

Write back ASAP.
JP

Juan Pablo hit send and looked around. Only one lady sat at the computer, her fingers flying over the keyboard. It took him almost three hours, but he finally completed four tutorials at the Khan Academy. Long ago, his abuela made him promise to always keep up his studies. He missed his violin fiercely. Normally, he would play for hours, but he could not play now. That would attract attention.

So, his fate was to swim all afternoon.

He slipped out into the air-conditioned hall. Blue carpet with gold crowns on it. He spotted an American penny and smiled as he picked it up. *It has become a cliché, but only because so many people who have lost a loved one discovers it. The Sky People set pennies or feathers in your path. Pennies for remembrance, feathers as a promise of reuniting . . .* He knew the way to the wave pool by heart.

He set his shopping bag and a towel neatly on a lounge chair.

One girl played in the pool. A boy sat on another lounge chair behind sunglasses, even though it was still early and the sun was soft. The girl dove under the waves and came out on the other side. She looked about Rocio's age. She had a round face with giant blue eyes. There was a smattering of freckles over her nose and cheeks. Water poured off her short brown hair.

Juan Pablo dove in and thinking of the baby whale, he swam under water to the far side and back again. He popped up near the girl. "Want to dive for a penny?"

"Okay. But only if you don't look where it goes."

"You can throw it."

She took the penny and turned her back to the pool. Juan Pablo did the same. She threw it and they dove. It was hard to see under water with the constant waves, and he wished he had the goggles from the *Catori*. Still, he spotted it on his first try and picked up the treasure.

The girl made a new rule. "Whoever finds it, the other person gets to throw it."

"Okay," Juan Pablo said.

The girl asked his name and he told her. "I'm Rory," she said.

"Can I play?" The boy rose from his chair.

"That's my twin brother, Cory. He cheats."

"I do not!"

The brother looked like his sister with the same round face, brown hair, and blue eyes. "I don't mind," Juan Pablo said.

Cory dove in. He came up near Juan Pablo and said, "Are you Mexican?"

"Cory, that's rude."

Juan Pablo did not know why this was rude. "Yes, I am."

"You don't look Mexican, but you sound kind of Mexican."

"Why don't I look Mexican?" Juan Pablo asked.

"Your eyes are so green," Rory said.

Juan Pablo smiled. "Your eyes are so blue."

"We're from California," Rory added. "San Diego, if you want to know exactly."

"Have you been to Disneyland?"

"Duh. Like a million times," Cory said. "My mom said she'd buy me an Xbox if I came on this stupid cruise."

Juan Pablo didn't think he understood. It sounded as if Cory's mom had to bribe him to go on this cruise, but that couldn't be right.

They played for a half-hour, but it was too easy. They decided to add three more pennies with the goal of whoever could get the most on a first dive. That proved more challenging.

They got ice-cream cones and sodas, which Juan Pablo savored.

The cruise was like a fantastic dream.

"The ship is so . . ." Juan Pablo thought of the English word meaning huge. "Enormous."

"Gigantic," Cory said.

"Humongous," Rory said.

"Wouldn't it be great for hide-and-seek?" Juan Pablo asked dreamily.

"That would be rad."

"Rad?" Juan Pablo didn't know that word.

"Great," Cory said. "Only how could you ever find anyone?"

"If you sent clues on your phone," Rory said.

"Let's do it." Cory leapt at the idea.

"I know, I know." Rory jumped up. "Give me ten minutes to hide. If you don't find me, I will send a text message with a clue."

Eager, even excited, Juan Pablo withdrew his iPad from his abuela's shopping bag.

Cory watched this. "You have a girl's purse."

Juan Pablo shrugged. "It is all I have."

"Weird." Cory grimaced with a shake of his head. "Are you gay?"

Juan Pablo greeted the question with confusion. He supposed he was gay, if he didn't think of what had happened and only thought of now. Rocio was safe in America and he was not afraid of being caught on the cruise ship. Not only did he have all the food he could eat, but a swimming pool and a theater and no school. But what did that have to do with his abuela's shopping bag?

Rory hit her brother. "That's not very polite."

Yet, the two twins stared at him, waiting for an answer.

"I am having fun, yes."

The twins exchanged glances. "But are you . . . like, gay—like, you know, queer?"

Queer? An English word meaning "not usual." Was he queer? He loved music and even math. He grew up in a butterfly sanctuary. His abuela was a medicine woman as well as a doctor and maybe one of the wisest people on earth. That might seem odd to other kids, but he would not use the word *queer*. "I don't think so. Do I seem queer to you?"

They shook their heads. "I've just never seen a boy with a purse."

"It was my grandmother's," Juan Pablo explained. "I need it to carry my iPad. I don't have a phone."

They turned to establishing rules for the game.

Though Cory protested, Rory went first. "She always goes first," Cory complained after she disappeared into the endless halls, rooms, and decks to hide. They gave her ten minutes to hide anywhere on the ship, except a cabin. She had to text hints every ten minutes.

The first hint came to Juan Pablo's iPad and Cory's phone:

Rory: *The same thing above me is below.*

The two boys stood by the poolside ice-cream stand.

"Huh?" Cory said.

Juan Pablo thought about it, but drew a blank.

JP: *We need another clue.*
Rory: *Can't see the ocean here.*

Juan Pablo reasoned out loud: "The only places without an ocean view are the halls."

The boys took off running. They burst from the elevator and raced down the lowest deck through the hall. Suddenly they were laughing, for no reason they knew.

No sign of Rory.

They popped back onto the elevator and went up to the next floor. They were racing down the hall, searching, when Juan Pablo thought of the other clue. "Wait." He stopped. "The same thing above as below?"

"The third and fourth decks are the same."

They raced back to the elevator and went to the third deck.

The returned to the elevator and rose to the fourth deck. They searched the halls, but they found nothing. Juan Pablo swung his iPad to see the next clue appear.

Rory: *No lazy people here.*

Cory blurted, "The gym."

"No, no," Juan Pablo said. "I have been there. The gym has an ocean view to pretend you are riding a bike into the ocean. It is very cool. I wanted to try, but it didn't look like it was for kids." He had always wanted a bike, but they were not practical in El Rosario with its steep hills.

It hit him. "The stairs. She is hiding in the stairs."

They played the game all afternoon and it was a blast.

Rory and Cory's parents were happy they were entertaining themselves, having fun and not bothering them, and so the three friends had dinner that night together. Afterward, they went to see the new movie, but all they could talk about was the game and the app they were going to make for everyone to play hide-and-seek with their phones. They would soon be rich.

Juan Pablo imagined paying Leonardo's medical school tuition, giving Rocio and her mom a new car and maybe even an American house. He could go to college and study music and entomology, which was his favorite dream besides playing first violin in a big-city symphony.

After the movie, and saying goodbye to Rory and Cory, he made his way to the casino to wait for BK to get off work. He peered inside the spacious room on the third deck. The wood paneling and red carpet kept it dark. Hanging lights cast the room in a dim glow. Only one couple sat at the bar. The roulette table, the slot machines, and poker and craps tables stood empty.

"Take a seat, kid. I just have to finish cleaning up."

Juan Pablo sat at a small corner table.

BK was talking to another crewman who was wiping down all the tables.

He withdrew his iPad to see an email from Rocio:

My mom is still in shock. My mom can't believe I am here. She keeps looking at the passport and birth certificate. She makes me tell her the story over and over. She keeps hugging me and crying. She is sad about her father but also happy I am finally with her in America; it is a miracle, she says. She thinks Elena arranged the whole thing from heaven.

My uncle heard about the murders at the cantina. It is all over the news. He left for El Rosario to get me immediately. He just got back. He is okay, so grateful I am safe.

Everyone is worried about you. I told them you were with the padre and he will take care of you until he finds a way to help you get to America, too. My mom wants you to call her as soon as possible. So call. I didn't tell her about the cruise ship because I didn't know if I should or not. I hate keeping a secret from her, but I don't want her to worry about you, too, especially if you're on a cruise.

Butterflies forever,
Rocio

PS: I have always dreamed of going on a cruise.

"Hey. Do I know you from somewhere?"

Relieved in the extreme that Rocio's uncle was okay after all, Juan Pablo looked up to see the young crewman staring at him. He was medium height and pudgy—one of Rocio's favorite English words, meaning not quite fat but almost fat.

Do I look pudgy, Juan Pablo? she would always ask, teasing, because she was so thin, which Mario always blamed on Elena's insistence that they never eat animals.

The man wore the same white coat and black bow tie of the evening dining crew. He had short dark hair and golden skin, but looked unfamiliar. His name tag said Julio. His small, round eyes stared at him with a strange intensity.

Juan Pablo shook his head. "I don't think so." His heart kicked in. The strange warning buzz sounded an alarm in his mind. He managed to shrug and pretended to work his iPad.

"Where are you from?"

"California. San Diego."

The man considered this before shaking his head. "I swear I know you from somewhere."

Juan Pablo forced a smile and added a shrug.

"Are you waiting for your parents or something?"

Juan Pablo started to answer, but BK suddenly appeared at his side. He put his hand on Juan Pablo's shoulder. "All done here. Let's go, kid." To Julio, he said, "I said I'd show him some magic tricks after my shift."

Julio laughed at this. "Show him the card tricks. That's worth something."

BK laughed as Juan Pablo rose and they exited together.

"Weird," was all BK said about it.

CHAPTER FOURTEEN

"Where's your mom and dad?" Rory asked the next day after they'd gone swimming and were eating lunch in the large dining hall. They had taken a table with a view of the ocean, surrounded by a hundred or more tables. A buffet covered the length of the auditorium-sized room, but after looking at the piles of food, they collectively decided to order grilled cheese sandwiches and sodas.

Juan Pablo smiled at their bloodshot eyes. "I am with my grandmother."

"Oh." Rory stared at her phone, texting a friend as she talked. "What cabin are you in?"

"2014."

"We're in a cheap cabin. No balcony," Cory said, the words somewhat muffled by the sandwich stuffed in his mouth.

Looking up, Rory sighed with the exaggeration of the much put-upon. "Mom wanted a balcony, but Dad said she has to learn we aren't as rich as her patients. Mom thinks she should be able to buy whatever she wants because she works so hard. She's a nurse for a plastic surgeon."

"Making people beautiful?"

"They just make 'em younger," Cory explained. "Our dad sells drugs. That's how they met."

Juan Pablo's eyes widened. "Your father sells drugs?" A droguista, here on the cruise?

"Yeah," Cory said. "For a big drug company, but he hates it. They keep hiring more people to do his job. So my dad makes less. He has a lot of stress. That's why he started drinking more, mom says."

"Do your parents fight a lot?" Rory asked.

"No. Never," Juan Pablo said.

"You're lucky. I hate it when they fight."

"Last night . . ." Cory shook his head, but didn't finish.

Rory confided, "We think they're going to get a divorce."

Rory and Cory exchanged looks of worry and sadness. Cory stopped eating and Rory brushed at her eyes, turning away. She stared out over the dining room.

Juan Pablo didn't know what to say.

"Why are those men staring at us?"

Juan Pablo turned to where Rory stared. The crewman, Julio, and another man stared at their table. Julio waved like they were friends. To Juan Pablo's horror, he marched over to their table.

"Hey, how's it going, buddy?"

Juan Pablo swallowed and not trusting himself, he took a long sip of soda. "Good."

"What's your name again? Juan Pablo?"

The buzzing was loud in his mind, but it seemed too late to lie, and he nodded.

"That's what BK said," Julio said.

Juan Pablo melted with relief. BK had told him his name.

"Just stopping by to say hello. Well, okay, Juan Pablo." He knocked his knuckles on the table. "Okay, now," he said again. "Have a fun day."

They watched Julio walk back to the other man. The two men conferred for several minutes before disappearing.

Juan Pablo breathed a sigh of relief.

The twins looked at each other and shrugged. "Come on," Cory said, rising. "Let's play the game. It's my turn. Give me ten minutes."

Cory disappeared out the main doors.

The next text came in.

Cory: *Look up. Blue.*

Rory and Juan Pablo studied the next clue, deciding Cory might be on the upper deck. They raced to the elevators.

"Rory, what is America like? To live there?" He didn't add, *where it is mostly, always, safe.*

"You've never been to America?"

Juan Pablo shook his head. "I have seen it on TV and in movies."

"I guess it is just like that. Only, you know, more real."

The more they played the game, the richer they were going to become; the game was more fun even than swimming. Everyone would want to play it, even adults, they decided. That night Juan Pablo ate dinner with Rory and Cory for the last time. They had spaghetti, french fries, and milkshakes. He had pie and cake for dessert and even though he was fuller than he ever had been, Juan Pablo savored his last free ice-cream cone. They spent three hours in the game room with other kids, making plans to connect online to keep working on their app, getting it ready for an investor.

Finally, they said goodbye.

Juan Pablo wanted to take one last swim in the pool.

There were a few other people in the Jacuzzi, but no one in the swimming pool. He floated on his back, staring up at the stars. Thinking of the Sky People and his abuela, he gave thanks for the fantastic voyage that took him straight to America's shores. He gave thanks for Rocio's safety. He gave thanks to his abuela for all the years she had been in his life.

He felt her love surround him. A physical warmth descended on him, filling him with peace and happiness, a feeling that everything would be all right.

"Te amo, Abuela," he whispered to the sky.

He finally forced himself out of the warm water. It was time to meet BK.

The warning buzz suddenly sounded in his mind. He hopped up and down, hoping it was water trapped in his ears, but no.

Cautioned by it, but not able to imagine anything wrong, he dried off and gathered his things. He made his way down to the casino. Few people were about at the late hour and most of these people collected in the casino, which closed at midnight.

The casino was empty. BK wiped down the bar, finishing up.

"Okay, kid, this is your last night. Tomorrow you will be in America. Are you ready?"

Juan Pablo nodded.

He had to wait a few minutes while BK completed the closing, but they soon made their way back to the theater where BK's cart was. No one questioned why he had to move the cart to his cabin every night. Juan Pablo hopped in. BK hummed as he pushed the cart to the employee elevator at the end of the ship.

Once down below, BK pushed the cart along the I-95. The crew members were all getting off of the late shift and there were a number of janitor carts and people carrying stacks of trays and linens.

"Hey, BK." Julio appeared from one of the side halls.

Juan Pablo froze instinctively, the buzzing suddenly loud in his mind.

"How's it going?" BK asked without stopping.

"You know that kid you were showing magic tricks to?"

"Yeah?"

"Look at this," Julio said.

Juan Pablo's heart pounded so loud, he feared it could be heard.

"What the fuck?" BK said.

"He's a wanted boy. Look at that reward."

BK pretended confusion. "I don't get it."

"There's a reward for information on his whereabouts."

BK whistled. "Geezus, who would pay that much for some kid?"

"Beats me," Julio said, smiling.

"You don't?"

"Me? Naw. These are the bad guys, you know? I don't get involved in any shit like that."

"How did you get it, though?" BK pressed.

"My wife's sister. She . . . I don't know . . . hangs with a certain type. It must have been passed on through her contacts. I knew I had seen that kid somewhere. Hey, I'm not supposed to mention this, but some shirts were asking around about you."

"Me?" BK asked.

"Wanted to know . . . how well you interact with the passengers. I guess there was a complaint about how the cards fall at your table. Numbers not adding up or something."

"Geezus," BK swore.

"No worries," Julio said. "It didn't seem serious. Just wanted to give you a heads-up."

They talked about the new contracts for a few minutes before BK headed quickly to his cabin. Juan Pablo jumped out of the cart. "What was it? What did he show you?"

BK ran his hands through the slicked-back red hair. "It was . . . well, it was like a wanted poster."

"With my picture?"

BK nodded.

"Do you really think he was telling the truth? That he didn't tell them where I am?"

BK grimaced. "I don't know. Uh, actually, I don't see that one walking away from two grand. But geezus, I might have my own problem."

Juan Pablo fell to the floor and dropped his head in his arms, trying to think what to do. He didn't know. If some crew member saw his picture, how many other people saw it? How long before he was caught?

BK withdrew a small bottle of liquor from a drawer. He drank it in one swallow, and for several long minutes, he was lost in his own thoughts before he noticed Juan Pablo again.

"Hey, hey. It doesn't mean anything."

Juan Pablo made no response.

"Look. Here's what you do, kid."

He looked up, eagerly awaiting this advice.

"Tomorrow I will roll this cart to a cab and put you in it. You'll go to the bus station."

"I have no money—"

"I'll buy you a ticket to—" He suddenly wondered, "Where are you going anyway? Do you know?"

Juan Pablo nodded. "I am meeting someone in Pacific Grove, California."

"Someone who will, like, look after you?"

Juan Pablo swallowed a small lie, nodding. Maybe it was someone who would look after him. He couldn't imagine who this would be, but he trusted Abuela. If no one was there, he would head for Rocio's mom's apartment in Arizona. Rocio's mom would help him, he knew.

"I'll tell you what I'll do. I'll buy you a ticket to Pacific Grove. Should only be eighty bucks or something. You get on the bus. You don't look back."

"Will you? Gracias, gracias. If only I could get there, I—"

"Hey. You're a special kid. No way I'm gonna let some group of thugs get their hands on you."

He patted Juan Pablo's shoulder. "Okay. Let's hit the sack, kid."

Juan Pablo soon fell into a troubled sleep. Three times he was awoken by a racing heart, the warning buzz in his mind, and strange dreams involving policemen.

He awoke to a burst of noise.

"Kid, get up!"

Juan Pablo started to get up. BK grabbed his arm and pulled him out from under the bunk, lifting him to his feet. "You got to get out of here!"

"But—"

"Go. Some shirts are coming. Someone complained." He snatched up Juan Pablo's violin and his backpack. "Said I cheated them. They're coming to search my cabin." He shoved the possessions into the boy's chest even as he pushed him to the door. "If they find you in here, we're busted. We'll both be history. Go, go, go. I'll catch up with you."

The door shut behind him.

Keeping his head down, Juan Pablo rushed down the main corridor, the I-95. He raced down the hall to the stairs. The corridor was crowded with crew members who stopped to stare at the young man rushing down the hall.

"Hey, kid," someone shouted behind him. "You're not supposed to be here."

Juan Pablo didn't stop. He reached the staircase and flung open the door. A sign read CREW MEMBERS ONLY, but he ignored it, taking the steps two at a time. Reaching the top, he stepped into the familiar hall of the cruise ship. All around him, passengers wandered down the hall, rolling suitcases over the carpeted floor.

The cruise ship had docked at San Diego's port. He was in America.

He quickly made his way to the main dining room. It was empty. He rushed out the hall and into the restroom.

It, too, was empty.

He tried to slow the race of his heart.

BK was in some kind of trouble, but it was not about him. No one knew he had been in BK's cabin. Any crew member who saw him probably thought he had just taken a wrong turn, maybe in his haste to disembark.

Everything was okay. He would just wait topside until BK located him. They would figure out how to get him into the cart and off the ship. It shouldn't be too hard.

It was okay, he told himself over and over.

His heart settled down. He used the toilet and as he brushed his teeth, he noticed that his hair was getting longer without his abuela's handy scissors. He smoothed it down. He looked normal again.

He found his way to the main deck. A long line of passengers waited to disembark. He went to the window to stare at his first sight of America.

A cloudy blue sky met the gray waters of the bay. Their giant ship docked in front of the modern blue and white cruise line building. He watched passengers meeting loved ones on the dock. Two policemen, wearing the navy blue uniforms of American police, stood on the dock. Arms folded and laughing, they, too, watched as the stream of passengers disembarked.

Juan Pablo marveled at how shiny and big and blue and clean everything looked. He turned back to the line. He watched the passengers pass by the ship's officers, nodding, saying goodbye, and moving on. Each passenger handed the officer an electronic card, which was swiped as they passed.

He did not have a card.

The line was getting shorter.

He returned to the empty hall.

He looked around nervously for BK.

Since so few people were left, he made his way to the stairs leading below deck. He cautiously made his way down and opened the door. The stairs opened to a narrower hall that fed the main corridor. The passageway was much quieter than normal. He peeked around the corner. Two crew members passed carrying piles of linen, that was all. He heard BK before he saw him.

"I can explain everything. I always carry that much cash—"

"You can tell it to the boss."

He could only see their backs. Two officers escorting BK down the hall.

Juan Pablo pressed against the wall before turning and heading up the stairs again. He opened the doors and stepped into the empty hall off the main deck.

He returned to the main deck where passengers were still lined up to disembark. Only thirty people left. He had no choice and nothing to lose.

He was last in line.

Nervously, looking this way and that, he caught sight of Cory and Rory running ahead of their parents. "Juan Pablo," Cory said. "Hey!"

Cory reached him first and stepped in line behind him.

"Are you waiting for us?"

"Yes," Juan Pablo said. "My grandmother went to get the car."

"Cool," Rory said, pulling a purple suitcase.

Cory and Rory's parents joined them. "Ah, Juan. Look at this. We are last off the boat. If you two ever woke before eight without sirens going off, I think I'd have a heart attack."

The twins' dad was tall and less overweight than just large. Big shoulders, a pleasant round face, and short-cropped hair.

"It's Juan Pablo, Dad," Rory corrected him as they moved up the line.

"Where's your grandmother?" the mom asked, looking around. "I want to congratulate her on raising a nice young man."

"Oh, she . . . well, she is up ahead already."

It seemed suddenly everyone was talking, but by this point, with only two passengers ahead, Juan Pablo couldn't hear, let alone comprehend any one word above the pounding of his heart and the loud buzz in his ears. Suddenly, he was staring at the officer's hand.

The officer waited for his card.

"I lost it."

"We can vouch for him," the twins dad said. "His grandmother has already gone off. He was waiting to say goodbye to the twins."

The two officers exchanged looks before moving to Rory and Cory, who both had their hands out.

"Do we get some kind of prize for being the last off the ship?" their dad asked as they went through the gate.

Juan Pablo stood on the other side. He stood in America.

Following Rory and Cory and their parents down the ramp and onto the dock, he almost laughed for his sudden joy. They passed the two policemen, who took no notice of him.

Everyone thought he was American now—that he belonged here.

A small group of people collected in front of the cruise building.

He spotted the boots first. The red boots.

His life came to a sudden, cruel end. He froze, waiting for an axe.

"Well, goodbye, Juan Pablo," Rory said. "We'll be looking for investors."

"I wish I had the money," Rory's dad added. "A hide-and-seek app. You'd swear there'd be one by now."

"Honey, can you get the car and bring it around?" Cory's mom said.

Juan Pablo looked at the two policemen.

The man with the red boots followed his gaze. He shook his head, as if to caution Juan Pablo not to do it, but the man with the red boots was not someone he listened to.

Juan Pablo headed right to the policemen.

He swallowed. "Excuse me, Mr. Policeman," he said, interrupting their conversation, and then said the hardest English words he could imagine: "I am Juan Pablo from El Rosario, Mexico, and I do not have the proper papers to be in America."

CHAPTER FIFTEEN

Abuela, you never told me . . .

This wasn't true, Juan Pablo realized as he sat surrounded by a thousand desperate children eating breakfast in the huge auditorium. She had told him many times. *Juan Pablo, no matter where you are in the world, you will find many people who are struggling, for no reason of their own making. You must always reach out and like I said, try to ease their burdens.* He just hadn't truly realized what she meant until now.

Most children ate silently, afraid to talk, not wanting to get in trouble with the adults watching over them. The adults seemed nice, but few spoke Spanish.

Housing over a thousand children, the shelter had been hastily set up by the government for some of the thousands and thousands of children crossing the border from Mexico into the United States.

"All of them, every one, desperate, young, and scared," he overheard a social worker lamenting.

Last night, Juan Pablo had slept in a bunk with another boy, Martin, from Guatemala. Quiet and shy, Martin had started praying in a whisper when the lights went out. Juan Pablo asked what was wrong. Trying to hold back tears, the story came out.

After losing both parents to pandilleros, or gang members, these bad men had given him the choice of either working for the gang killing rivals or being killed. Martin and his older brother, Lucus, had no option but to set off to find their grandfather in Los Angeles. They had no money or food, and they had to beg. Sometimes people were generous, sometimes not. Sometimes they had food, but often they didn't. One night they had fallen asleep behind a small auto repair shop in Oaxaca. When Martin woke, his brother was gone. He spent two weeks looking for him. He prayed with all his heart that he would find his brother waiting for him at his grandfather's in Los Angeles.

Thinking of all the heartache in one room, Juan Pablo finished the bowl of oatmeal, but noticed the girl next to him kept wiping tears from her large brown eyes. The little girl's oatmeal remained untouched.

Noticing this, a lady guard stepped forward. The guard's overweight form spilled out of the too-tight guard uniform. She had large eyes, rimmed in black like a raccoon, and bright red lipstick accented the thin lines of her mouth. Written in messy cursive, her name tag read Margo. She looked angry and sounded mean.

"Don't like the food?"

The little girl froze, staring hard at the bowl of oatmeal.

"What's wrong with you?"

Juan Pablo asked quietly, "The lady wants to know if you are all right."

The little girl shook her head.

"What is wrong?" Juan Pablo asked in Spanish.

A small hand went to her cheek. "My tooth hurts. I want my mom."

Juan Pablo translated this. The woman looked at him. "You speak English?"

"Yes," Juan Pablo said.

"Tell her she is in luck. The American taxpayers will probably love to send her to a dentist." The woman wandered off.

Juan Pablo spoke to the little girl. "What's your name?"

"Lila."

"Lila, these people will try to find your mother for you. They will help you. They are good people. They will send you to a dentist to fix your tooth."

She nodded, but said nothing else. Too scared. Everyone was scared like that.

Later Juan Pablo played soccer with the other boys his age in the cement yard outside, surrounded by high barbed-wire fencing. A moist fog billowed between the sky and the ground, painting the world gray. He had heard of fog his whole life, but this was his first experience of the mist.

Juan Pablo couldn't concentrate. He kept searching the surrounding area for the man with the red boots. What would happen if he came here? Could he find him here? If he found him on the cruise ship, he could find him anywhere.

Would the Americans turn him over?

He didn't think so, but there was no telling what the man with the red boots would do to get him. He'd had another nightmare last night. He was being chased, running for his life, looking for his abuela and Rocio. The man was gaining on him . . . He woke in a panic. At first he didn't know where he was, but in the darkness, he heard someone crying. Then he remembered.

Finally giving up on the game, he retreated to the sidelines with the other children to think. If only he could play his violin, he felt he would be okay, but they had taken his violin and iPad from him for safekeeping. They also wouldn't let him contact Rocio on his iPad. Not until he was "processed," whatever that was.

He tried to play the music in his mind, but even this was hard.

The fog began dissipating, chased by a noonday sun that reached warm fingers to the asphalt. The heat was comforting. Sunshine made him think of the butterflies, and that gave him courage. He had lost everything and he had nothing more to lose. He might as well ask again.

He approached the lady watching over them. Short, with short brown hair and large dark glasses, she offered him a smile. Her name tag said Judy.

"Excuse me, Ms. Judy," he beckoned politely. "I have a question."

She brightened with a smile. "Ohmygod. You speak English?"

"Yes. I was wondering if my violin and iPad are safe. They were taken from me for safekeeping and I was hoping I could check on them. When it is not too much trouble."

Judy stared in dumbfounded wonder.

But Juan Pablo didn't notice Judy's stare for several long seconds. He was watching a monarch butterfly floating behind a woman who emerged from a white car. She clicked the electronic lock. Thick gray curls framed a warm and kind face. He knew she was kind from a distance, though he could not say how he knew. She wore a blue and green flowing top over loose-fitting pants. She carried an enormous purse, one that reminded him of Rocio's favorite old movie, *Mary Poppins*. The thought panged his heart. The girl loved that old movie; she made him learn all the songs and then made him play them over and over.

Judy waved to the lady and she started walking toward them.

"Hi, Dolores," Judy said, like they were friends. "There's a long line of kids already. Emphasis on long."

"Tell me they found an interpreter. Otherwise, I can't see what good I can do here."

Judy looked from Dolores to Juan Pablo. "What's your name, young man?"

"Juan Pablo."

"Dolores, you're in luck. You won't believe this, but this young man here, Juan Pablo, just informed me—in perfect English—that we are holding his violin in custody and that he would like to visit it."

Dolores Goodman absorbed this and laughed. "I see. So, you play the violin?"

"Yes," Juan Pablo said.

"Hmm . . ." Dolores said.

He felt the intensity of her stare.

"Who is your favorite composer?"

His favorite composer? There was no harder question, for the answer changed with the hour. "That is a very difficult question," he said. "I love Beethoven most, of course, I guess, but I also love Bach, Mozart, and lately I have found that I love Mendelssohn very much. Before this I was very drawn to Debussy. I think his music is very exciting."

Dolores's smile grew in stages. "And who is your favorite violinist?"

"That is hard, too. Sarah Chang is excellent, but Joshua Bell. I once saw him perform in Mexico City."

Dolores studied him with intense curiosity and an amused smile. She asked a number of basic questions as they stood there in the hall before she asked, "And are you good in school, Juan Pablo?"

"My grandmother took me out of school. We bought an iPad instead, so I could do math at the Khan Academy—"

"The Khan Academy? My grandkids use them. What level math are you at?"

"Calculus."

"But how old are you?"

He told her, then continued, "My grandmother insisted I do at least one math tutorial a day, but I love math almost as much as music and I normally do four. I also take violin lessons from Señor Grendal in Iceland."

"On Skype?" When he nodded, she said, "Juan Pablo, what if we go visit your violin? I suspect I'd love to hear you play."

"I would be most honored."

Dolores threw her head back and laughed. "I knew I agreed to leave my happy retirement for a reason."

That was the beginning of their relationship. With thick gray hair, old-fashioned glasses, and bright, colorful clothes, Dolores Goodman, he soon learned, had come all the way from San Francisco to help process the children here. It was his second week at the naval station.

Juan Pablo had never met anyone like Dolores. Being her interpreter was the saddest job in the world.

Eight years old and scared, Rosa Ochoa wore a pink hairband that kept slipping over her forehead. She pushed it back but kept her round, large eyes on her lap. Speaking in a whisper, she answered Dolores's questions as best she could.

"Where's she from, Juan Pablo?" Dolores asked, not looking up.

Before he could answer, she held up her finger. "Yes," the older woman said, speaking into the phone now. "I'm looking for Carman Garcia. Is she there?"

Juan Pablo marveled at Dolores's ability to orchestrate the phones, computer, and children all at the same time. They had become friends over the last two weeks. Dolores and her large family loved music, too. She had seen many of the greats perform live.

"I love Dudamel. It is my dream to see him perform someday."

"That is a lovely dream, Juan Pablo. He is fabulous, electrifying!"

"You have seen him in real life?"

"Many times. My whole family goes whenever we can."

"I have seen him on YouTube, but they say it is not the same."

"No, there is nothing like a live performance. Maybe someday I can take you."

Dolores was an abuela herself and all three of her children and all six of her grandchildren played instruments. Her daughter-in-law was even a music history professor at Stanford University where she studied the great composers' lives. This was fascinating to Juan Pablo; of course, he had read about each of the great composers on Wikipedia.

He told her about his abuela's passing and about Rocio. Dolores had called Rocio's mother immediately, and she let him talk to Rocio, so she wouldn't be worried. Unfortunately, it was against the law to let him go to "friends;" placements had to be blood relatives. She said he was a very special case and would have a special placement, but in the meantime, she needed his help with the other children.

He did not tell her about the man with the red boots. He didn't want to frighten her, nor did he want to place her in danger. Still, ever since he'd met Dolores, he had stopped having nightmares.

"Did she leave a forwarding address?" Dolores inquired into the phone. "I've got her two kids here, and believe me, they are anxious to see their mother."

The older woman wrote down an address and hung up. She Googled this new address as she motioned for Juan Pablo to continue.

"Rosa is from Atlántida—"

"Where?" Dolores asked.

"Honduras," Juan Pablo explained.

"Father?"

"Rosa's father was a policeman."

"Her father is in Honduras? Does she have a number?"

"He was killed. Murdered."

Dolores looked up finally. "Murdered? Who killed him? Does she know?"

"The bad guys," Juan Pablo conveyed her words.

"Again. The ubiquitous bad guys. Mother?"

"Her mother is a house painter in Washington."

"DC or state?"

Juan Pablo asked Rosa, but he already knew her answer. Sure enough, he said, "She just says Washington in America."

"Please tell me she has another relative."

Juan Pablo asked Rosa, but he already knew this answer as well. "Her abuela, her grandmother, but—"

"Excellent. In Honduras?"

"No," Juan Pablo said. "It is another sad story, Dolores. She said the bad men kept calling her mother in America for money so they wouldn't hurt her and her abuela, but the price kept going up and when her mother could no longer pay, her mother told them to come to America, no matter how hard it was. Rosa left Honduras with her abuela."

"And where is this grandmother now?"

Juan Pablo whispered, "She didn't make it. She died on the way."

Dolores finally looked at Rosa. "The poor kid. What happened? Does she say?"

Juan Pablo shrugged. Both he and Dolores had heard the same story dozens of times. Walking for days and days. No food, sometimes no water. Finding the "beast," which was the slang name for the trains running north. Trying to run and catch a bar to jump on—no easy feat for a grown man, let alone a little girl and an old abuela.

"Rosa says it was always hard getting on and off the train. They sat on top, hanging on with all their strength. It was very windy. There were many other children on the trains, but she never talked to them, except to show them her bruises and cuts. Everyone was afraid of dying and they were always so hungry and thirsty. Her abuela finally couldn't walk anymore and she paid the last money to some men to take Rosa across the border."

Juan Pablo didn't say what happened then, because Rosa couldn't say. She tried, but she just started crying.

Rosa wiped at her eyes and spoke softly to Juan Pablo.

"She wants to see her mother."

"Oh, honey," Dolores said, "I will do everything possible to find your mom."

Juan Pablo translated this and Rosa wiped at her eyes, nodding.

Dolores was punching out a new number for the Garcia girls. "Juan Pablo, see if you can get anything more on the address."

Juan Pablo asked Rosa if she was given anything, especially a number or an address to reach her mom. Rosa nodded, but hesitated. Juan Pablo assured her she was safe, that Dolores was a good woman, an abuela herself. She had six grandchildren; Juan Pablo had seen the pictures.

Rosa removed her hairband. She handed this to Juan Pablo. The number was written in a black marker on the underside.

"I got it, Dolores. She has a phone number."

"Hallelujah. Uno momento," she said as she waited on the phone.

Soon three more children would be reunited with their mothers.

For more than two weeks, every day was the same. He woke up, showered when his group was called, ate breakfast, and then found Dolores in her office. Children were called in, and he translated their stories for Dolores. The goal was always to reunite children with a relative in the United States or their home country.

During lunch and after work, he and Dolores went to the room that housed his violin. He was able to play as much as time permitted. When Dolores was tired—they worked very long hours—she often lay down on a couch and closed her eyes to listen. She always recorded his music. "I play it for my family and a few friends, too. Lisa, my daughter-in-law, is so impressed, Juan Pablo. She can't wait to meet you."

The idea that he would meet the professor of music excited him, but he said nothing. His abuela always said, *Some people say things that aren't true just to make people happy. Sadly, the happiness ends when the truth appears.* He didn't think Dolores was this kind of person, but the idea of meeting a real-life music professor seemed impossible.

"Where will I go when I leave?" Juan Pablo had asked, reasonably enough.

"Depends," she had told him. "I am working on it. You have a court date. Ultimately, a judge will decide."

His court date was supposed to be tomorrow, but it had been postponed again. He suspected Dolores of arranging this delay because she needed an interpreter.

"You are a godsend," Dolores said more than once. "I really believe that."

"I am happy to help."

"That might be the most special part."

The more he knew Dolores, the more he came to care for her. She was not at all like his abuela, but she had his abuela's same kindness. She let him call Rocio once a day. She had brought him three books to read. *To Kill a Mockingbird* was his favorite. She arranged for him to have his iPad while she supervised so he could exchange emails and texts with Rocio, who loved being with her mother again and loved her new school. Dolores played music while they worked. Lisa sent her the very best music with interesting bits of information.

Dolores loved sharing stories about her family. Dolores's husband, Sam, was a professor like her daughter-in-law, but of psychology. Her oldest daughter, Laura, was a veterinarian, and she was married to Lewis, a doctor. They had three children: Mark, fifteen, who loved sports and girls; Kyle, thirteen, who loved astronomy; and little Eva, a "special needs kid," who Dolores said was a conduit for love. *Conduit* meant a conductor. Eva was a conductor of love. Dolores's other daughter, Kimberly, was a schoolteacher. She was married to Doug, a computer scientist at Google, and they had three children: Chris, eight, a baseball player; Maureen, the math whiz; and little Sam, who was not so little, though only two years old. Sam had been named after Dolores's son who had died some two years ago.

"He passed away like your mom and your abuela," she explained in voice softened by loss. "A mother is not supposed to have favorites among their children, but . . ."

She didn't finish, but Juan Pablo could guess the end to the sentence. "I am sorry, Ms. Dolores. I truly am. My abuela said losing a child is the hardest thing on earth until—"

He stopped, unsure if he should say the rest.

"Until what, Juan Pablo?"

"Until . . . well, she said until you experience gratitude."

Dolores was taken aback. "Gratitude for your child's death?"

Juan Pablo shook his head. "No, no. Gratitude for having known their love."

Dolores just stared, and for several minutes he tensed with the certainty that he had said the wrong thing. But finally he noticed her eyes were wet with tears. She removed her glasses and wiped them. He could tell Dolores understood what his abuela said, but she never responded.

Finally, he asked, "Do you believe in the Sky People?"

"The Sky People?"

"The people who live in the spirit realm after they die on earth."

She thought about it for a long time. "I don't know. I want to believe that. More than anything."

"My abuela also always said belief in something often makes it true."

Dolores took that in and rose. She came to where he was standing and hugged him. Her hug, a grandmother's, stayed with him a long time.

The man with the red boots seemed so far away now.

CHAPTER SIXTEEN

The guard Margo held a clipboard and appeared to be reading from it. "Juan Pablo?"

Juan Pablo turned to see the woman standing at the door to the dormitory. She seemed nervous, her gaze darting this way and that, the anger hiding behind her thick makeup. The other day he had heard her complaining about "freeloaders," these people from other countries who stole from the hard-working people of this one. "The damn government squeezing us to give them a free ride . . ."

The buzzing in his ears warned him of something terrible happening, but what could it be? Dolores wasn't here yet. Most of the children had been sent to relatives. Some unfortunates had been deported back to their countries, but only when they had relatives who would take them in and keep them safe. At least that was the intention. They were closing the naval station shelter soon.

Juan Pablo set down his book and looked up. "Yes? Is Dolores here?" Normally Dolores fetched him herself.

"That is not your business, is it? The bus is leaving. You need to hurry up."

Juan Pablo looked around in a panic. There were only a couple of hundred children left. Only about two dozen kids waited in his dorm now, down from eighty-seven.

They hadn't even been called to their showers or breakfast yet.

"Where am I going?"

"Just gather your things and come with me."

Juan Pablo swept up his backpack and swung down from the bunk. Some children said goodbye, but most of them just watched anxiously.

"Where am I going?" He asked again as he followed the woman out.

"An orphanage in Mexico has agreed to take you."

Juan Pablo stopped with a great shock upon hearing these words. The jolt quickly gave way to a loud and long *no* in his mind. "I can't go back." He shook his head. "First, I am to see a judge and—"

"A judge has already ruled. You're going back." She added, "You shouldn't have come in the first place."

"But Dolores said—"

The woman's hand came to his arm, dragging him forward. "Dolores isn't in charge. I am, and you're on the list of children to be deported today."

"There's a mistake. I can't go back—"

The woman kept moving, shoving him forward. "There's no mistake. All the Mexican minors with no parents here are going back to Mexico today."

He was the only minor from Mexico now.

"But . . . but, then I need my iPad and my violin—"

The woman tightened her hand around his as she led him out the doors and into a foggy morning where a small yellow school bus waited at the curb.

"Please, my violin—"

"I don't know anything about that. All I know is you are supposed to be on that bus there."

He couldn't believe this was happening. There must be a mistake.

"Dolores took my violin to keep it safe. It's in the break room where they keep these things—down the hall. I can't leave without it. I can't live without it and my iPad, too—"

The doors to the bus opened. The driver, an enormous man, looked stern, menacing somehow, not a normal bus driver. "Darse prisa," he said in Spanish. "I've got a long drive."

"But you don't understand—"

"Look, kid," the woman said, her face reddening, "I don't have time for this, believe me. If there really is some violin, we'll mail it to the orphanage—"

"It is not to be mailed. It is very valuable, priceless even. You don't understand. I can't go without my violin—"

The woman's hand tightened around his, hurting him now, squeezing. Finger pointing, eyes full of fury, she spoke slowly. "I am sick and tired of you people thinking you can just waltz into our country and take advantage of us. Well, you can't! You are illegal. You are going back one way or another. That's the law."

"Please, please, if you would just call Dolores, she will explain. It is not fair—"

The bus driver came down the steps. "I can handle him." The man was the same height as Juan Pablo, but twice the weight. Juan Pablo searched his face, but saw only anger. Why was he mad? He started to shake his head, to speak, but the man grabbed Juan Pablo's backpack. He tried to hold on to it, but it was snatched away and tossed onto the bus.

Shaking his head, knowing something was terribly wrong, Juan Pablo backed up, but the huge man sprang forward and punched him. Hard in the stomach. The air left his body with an unnatural noise. Pain shot through him. Colors suddenly left his field of vision and he started to fall over. The man's arms came around him and with a sick grunt and no small effort, he lifted Juan Pablo onto the bus. With a hard shove, he pushed Juan Pablo onto the floor.

The driver barked out the Spanish words, "Sit down. And I better not hear a word from you the whole way."

"Where's the rest of my money?" Margo called. "You're supposed to pay me—"

The driver ignored this and shut the doors.

Gasping, feeling pain throughout his body, Juan Pablo tried to stand. He fell into a seat. His hand went to his mouth to stop from crying. His violin, his violin, his violin, he was losing his violin. He suddenly understood a fate much worse than even the man with red boots. He would be nothing and no one.

He called out to the Sky People for help.

Still, like blood from a wound, hope drained from him with each passing mile. The driver never looked at him, never said a word. The cities fell away in a blur of concrete and green and white freeway signs: Ventura, Oxnard, Los Angeles, Long Beach. He caught sight of the Disneyland sign and his heart sank further.

Rocio. He closed his eyes and pictured her with her mother. They would be strolling in a park, making plans. Fantastic American plans. A good school, books, and new clothes, all signaling a happy ending. He tried to focus on this, on Rocio's happy ending.

If he could just talk to her now. She would move heaven and earth to see that his violin was safe, to see it returned to him. She alone knew what his violin meant to him. It was his life.

Somehow, someone would help him contact Rocio.

He felt even this small hope disappear as the bus crossed the Mexican border. The border guard waved them through the crossing. The bus sped up, crossing lanes to the right.

Where America was sparkling and orderly, Mexico's boisterous pandemonium was colorful and chaotic. The sights of Tijuana came as an assault to his senses. The brightly painted buildings, the crowded streets, the famous bull-fighting ring. To the left el gueto—the ghetto—spread over the hillside like a haphazard collage of building frenzy, cardboard and metal siding put together in a jumbled collection of dwellings. To the right dozens of auto repair shops and dentist offices that served mostly American customers bravely looking for a bargain.

Less than a hundred meters from the border, the bus pulled over and came to a stop on the side of the freeway. Juan Pablo stared at his awful fate. There was no orphanage.

The man with the red boots waited for him.

"No, no," he whispered as a terrible fear engulfed him. He backed up even as the bus driver rose and turned to get him.

"Vamoose!"

But he was too frightened to move, except to back against the window, shaking his head.

A large, thick hand came to his arm and he was roughly pulled forward and pushed hard. He fell to his hands and knees, hitting his shoulder. Pain shot through his upper body, but it was nothing when laid alongside his fear. The big man reached down, pulled him up, and shoved him down the short flight of steps. Juan Pablo fell hard on his knees. He scrambled to get up.

"Don't even think of running, amigo."

Juan Pablo slowly stood. The loud ringing in his ears drowned out the noise of cars whizzing by. He drew the fumes deep in his lungs. His heart thumped too fast, as if trying to escape the small confines of his chest. He felt the tremble in his upper lip. It shot down his arms and hands as he clutched at the pain shooting from his shoulder.

The bus driver tossed his backpack out of the bus. It hit the wire fence and fell down.

Juan Pablo's gaze went from the red boots, to the Levi's, to the blue work shirt and tan hat. The man had no facial hair and a large unsmiling mouth. Dark glasses hid his eyes. Up close, he looked surprisingly ordinary.

Juan Pablo knew this was a deception. Still, he thought to explain. "I didn't mean to kill them. They were going to hurt my friend. I had to stop them. I had to. The poison, it was too much, but . . ." He didn't mean to kill them. He had only wanted to stop them. "I had to stop them."

The Hunter nodded as if he understood. "And now you have to pay the price."

Juan Pablo shook his head. In a whisper, "I don't want to die." As he said the words, he felt how true it was.

"It always amazes me how desperately people cling to it." His gaze swept their dismal surroundings. "This absurd sweat and struggle over hollow crumbs."

These words were said with a soul-numbing disgust. Juan Pablo didn't understand. "But . . ." He grasped for a reason, for something to make sense. "Why—"

"Why?"

Juan Pablo sensed but didn't see the man's sudden bemusement this question posed. "There is no why," he explained. "That's the whole point. I just deliver people to their destination a bit sooner than expected." He looked at the black Cadillac waiting by the side of the road. "If you want to take that, pick it up." His head motioned to the backpack.

Juan Pablo's gaze went to his familiar backpack. His heart was pounding crazily and he could barely think. The only things in his backpack were the milkweed seeds for the . . . "Butterflies . . ."

"Butterflies," the man repeated mysteriously, as if it were an unfamiliar word being tested for the first time.

The red boots walked over to the waiting car and he opened the trunk, motioning for Juan Pablo to get inside.

The boy started to shake his head.

"I can deliver you dead. Less pay, but probably less trouble."

The simple statement stopped him. Poised for flight, but held to the spot by the warning. Juan Pablo studied the fast-moving cars.

I can deliver you dead . . . This couldn't be the end. Would anyone notice a boy being forced into a trunk? Would it matter if they did?

No, he realized, and the Hunter knew it.

The first tenuous step felt as if it covered the distance of a mile.

He stumbled with the second step, hating himself for it. He struggled to get up.

He heard the click of the revolver over the irregular pounding of his heart, the warning roar in his ears, and the deafening thunder of the traffic. He slowly stood. He forced each foot in front of the other until he stood at the back of the Cadillac, staring into the trunk.

The blow came hard and swift, knocking him face-down into the trunk. In one swift movement, the man lifted his legs into the trunk and shut the lid.

No one heard Juan Pablo's shocked cry into the dark.

He felt the motion of the tires beneath him as the car gathered speed. Pain continued to ricochet through his shoulders. He shook uncontrollably. All he could think was he did not want to die.

He was not ready to join the Sky People. Not until he had heard the London Philharmonic play Beethoven's Seventh. Not until he witnessed Dudamel conduct Mahler's Fifth or had seen Joshua Bell play again. Not until he had mastered all the great music on earth. He wanted to go to a music school with other young musicians who were like him, who were born with the music inside like butterflies in their pupas.

He wanted so badly to live.

There were so many other dreams screaming for attention, protesting this fate. Rocio and he were forever creating and adding to a long list of all the things they wanted to do. Travel to all the great cities, go to university, learn how to scuba-dive, ride a hot air balloon into the stratosphere, climb the tallest mountains on each continent and the tallest buildings in China and America. They wanted to rescue elephants in Africa, turtles in the Galápagos, homeless dogs in Mexico City. They wanted to eat in Google's employee café and at the top of the Eiffel Tower, tour Chartres, witness the northern lights, visit Stonehenge, and stand at the southernmost tip of Chile, where Rocio swore they would dance with penguins.

These thoughts passed too quickly to fully grasp. Fear fueled his pounding heart, quick breaths, and shaking.

His abuela's voice sounded in his mind: *The poor old man was literally shaking with a terrible fear. A fear of dying.*

He felt a prick in his side and reached down to feel his pocket. With no small effort he managed to remove his abuela's treasured butterfly pin. He held it tightly.

Help me, Abuela. Please help me.

Fear is only good when it keeps you from danger. Once the danger is upon you, it turns on you and hurts you.

But how can you stop being afraid if you are afraid?

Oh, there are many tricks. You can accept the worst that will happen. Once you accept the worst, the very worst, the fear abandons you.

Death. He was going to die.

Just as death is not to be courted, it is also a foolish thing to fear. Especially for those souls who understand that this life is a temporary shell that was borrowed for a short time on earth before we return to our place among the Sky People. But death is not to be feared even for those ignorant of the Sky People, those who believe death causes you to just cease. Think of it this way: billions upon billions of people have done it; it cannot be that bad.

Juan Pablo confronted his death.

If he simply ceased to be, if he just went kaput, he would no longer know all that he missed. His imagined future would cease to exist, too, as if it never were. There was no pain or suffering or anything. There was nothing.

Or, he would be joining the Sky People . . .

Do the Sky People have music, Abuela? he once asked.

His abuela threw her head back and laughed. *Music is how God talks to us. You, of all people, know this, Juan Pablo. Music surrounds the Sky People.*

As if on cue, he suddenly became aware of a distant symphony. Not just any symphony, but Mozart's Forty-First Symphony, a favorite. It seemed impossible, but the music emanated from the car—the Hunter was listening to Mozart.

Or was he? Was this just his imagination?

But how can I accept death when I want so badly to live?

What if the poor earthbound pupa knew he was becoming the butterfly, that his destiny waited in the endless bounty of the sky? All worries and fears would be replaced by a great and powerful joy and freedom.

Comforted by his abuela's words, he tried to focus on the distant hint of Mozart's symphony. He pictured the music rising in notes to the sky. He had played the violin's concerto many times. He imagined playing it now . . .

In his mind's eye, as if to save him the terror, Mozart carried him to a place far beyond thought, a place of pure feeling. Time disappeared completely.

He was saved.

Just as the last crescendo rose and Juan Pablo felt his fingers stretch and lift and flex over the last chords, a screech and a boom burst upon the small space. The Cadillac took a sharp swerve. He was thrown against the back. He jolted into a renewed panic.

The buzzing returned with a vengeance.

Juan Pablo froze, waiting for what would happen next.

The car door opened and shut. Juan Pablo heard boots against gravel.

The trunk opened. Sunlight assaulted him and forced his eyes shut. When he opened them, he found himself staring at the Hunter. "Out." He motioned with a flip of his head.

With no small effort, Juan Pablo got out.

His thoughts tumbled into confusion before supplying an understanding of the scene before him. The Cadillac had a flat tire. The Hunter rifled through the trunk, lifting a latch to get at a spare and a jack. He said nothing, but then there was nothing to say. It was merely a brief stop on the way to ending his short life.

The car rested on the side of a huge field of tall green plants six feet high. A strange pungent scent filled the air, familiar but not. The field of emerald stretched in all directions on both sides of the road as far as the eye could see. A small mountain chain rose in the far distance on the other side.

They could not be far from Tijuana. How long had he been in the trunk? Not more than two hours, maybe less.

A chemical smell mixed with the strange scent of the plants. Pesticides. Killer of butterflies and everything else that lived in the sky or crawled on the ground. *Every year there are fewer butterflies, but also other insects. I don't think the farmers realize what kills one insect, kills everything, including finally the very crop they are trying to protect . . .*

The Hunter removed a jack, a crowbar-like tool, and a much smaller spare tire. Juan Pablo might have been a suitcase for all the attention he got. The man let the tire and the crowbar fall at Juan Pablo's feet and took the jack around to the flat tire on the other side.

The buzzing in Juan Pablo's ears grew louder, warning him of danger—which was not necessary. He could not be more aware of it. His heart beat in a slow, steady, and very loud beat, like the beginning of Beethoven's Ninth Symphony. Was he supposed to just stand there, waiting to be put back in the trunk and carried off to his death?

He shielded his eyes from the sun as he looked across the field of leafy plants stretching up beneath the arch of blue sky. He realized even before he saw it, the signal to run, because his body was so tense, poised for flight. He gave no clue as the Hunter went about the business at hand and one side of the car began to lift up.

A butterfly floated slowly across the road and flittered invitingly over the tall field of marijuana plants. His heart leapt. He almost laughed. He did not run. He quietly—in the same way he managed not to wake his abuela while she slept—oh so quietly, disappeared into a field of green.

However it came out, like a butterfly to the warmth of a summer's sun, he was moving to freedom.

The Cadillac lifted and the Hunter went to retrieve the spare.

The young man was gone.

A gun manifest in his hand, he gave a low, amused chuckle. The Hunter jumped up onto the roof of the Cadillac.

The sun, sinking in the west, blinded him. Shielding his eyes, the Hunter watched and waited.

The boy was unnaturally smart. There was no sign.

He aimed where he imagined the boy was.

A bullet shot passed Juan Pablo's ear. Juan Pablo froze, holding perfectly still for several tense moments.

The Hunter was just guessing at his location.

Head lowered, he moved with quiet, stealthy deliberation through the tall plants. The Hunter would look for the slightest disturbance in the field. Ducking between plants, careful not to brush so much as a leaf, he crept forward. After twenty plants, he turned left again. He counted nine plants before turning forward again for twenty. Then thirty-two plants left.

Juan Pablo slowly zigzagged this way and that, but moved steadily north.

He tiptoed straight ahead, counting plants as if notes on a musical score, creating a chaotic imaginary maze.

The sweep of machine-gun fire sounded from a great distance away. The painfully familiar sound continued for several long minutes. Juan Pablo never looked back. He knew what it meant.

The Hunter was desperate. He had no idea where he was.

Juan Pablo headed in the opposite direction. He started running, unmindful of disturbing plants because he was so far away. The occasional machine-gun fire sounded further and further away.

After a half-hour or so, Juan Pablo stopped and listened.

Nothing and no one stirred. Giant marijuana plants shot up to the sky in neat rows as far as the eye could see. Breathing heavily, he tried to think what the man with the red boots would do now.

He would probably return to the Cadillac and begin circling the fields. He would search for the slightest sign or color among the green.

He tried to think what to do. Which direction was safest?

Ignoring his growing thirst and hunger as best he could, he waited—he didn't how long he sat there in the middle of the marijuana field, a half-hour, maybe more. But at some point he stood up. Just in time to see a butterfly floating northwest.

He started off. He walked through the endless fields for hours. Roads appeared and he dashed across, disappearing into the sameness on the other side. Kilometers of marijuana fields.

He spotted the people in the far distance, farm workers in a field. He turned away and put a meter of green plants between them. At last he reached the end of the field, marked by a chainlink fence crowned with barbed wire. He walked alongside it for another kilometer and then turned back inside the protection of the green sea.

Fighting a terrible thirst, he finally noticed the sun had begun sinking toward the horizon and the shadows of the plants lengthened. Occasionally a dirt road interrupted the endless rows of plants, but there was still no end in sight. One marijuana field could not be this long, could it?

He eventually came to a slight incline, like a gently rolling hill. The marijuana plants climbed right up. He considered following them, but there was a danger to standing on a hill and looking across. So he turned right instead.

At last the rows of plants opened onto a wider dirt road. The green fields continued on the other side. He looked up and down. Empty. Keeping hidden in the plants, he followed the road toward the setting sun.

He heard the noise before he saw it. An old yellow farm truck headed toward him. He stopped to watch it pass. Field workers sat in the back of the old truck. He heard them singing before they passed. He knew the folk song well; his abuela loved to sing it when she was working.

Love, love, love
born in you, born in me
from hope
Love, love, love
born of God, for two
born from the soul . . .

Juan Pablo took it as a sign. He stepped out. The song stopped with the truck.

The driver looked ancient: old, weathered brown skin, gray hair. Bent over the steering wheel, he squinted at the boy.

"Amigo, what the heck are you doing out here in the middle of nowhere?" The old man's voice was surprisingly cheerful. "Stealing a little zacate?"

"No, no." He tried to think of a plausible lie, but nothing came to mind. Fatigue threatened to pull him under, far greater than his monstrous thirst. Just this morning he was safe at the shelter in America waiting for Dolores to show up. Then he was thrown on a bus, forced to leave his violin for the first time in his life, taken back to Mexico, and handed over to the man who would see him killed for saving Rocio. He escaped with his life, dodging bullets and a man with supernatural powers to hunt people.

Exhaustion and worry claimed him. He could barely stand. He felt suddenly close to tears. Too tired to lie, he uttered the strange and awful truth. "I am running from a man who wants to kill me."

The old man absorbed the veracity of the simple statement in an instant. They all were familiar with this hard reality that claimed so many innocents in these troubled times. He glanced uncertainly back at his friends. Another man asked reasonably, "Why would someone want to kill you?"

Juan Pablo no longer wanted to be separated from the truth. "His men were responsible for my abuela's death and my best friend's abuelo's death. They were going to hurt her, Rocio, whom I love, who I have always loved. I couldn't let them. I poisoned them and they died. Now, they want revenge."

"El cielo te ayude," the old man muttered.

Heaven help him indeed.

The other men cursed, spit, shook their heads. One swore, "La maldición del dios banditos."

"We can get you to Tijuana," the old man said, motioning to the others. Two men, younger, brown, and lean from a life of fieldwork, reached strong arms down. Juan Pablo felt himself lifted onto the truck. Two other men parted and made room for the boy on one side. They asked for his name and he told them before collapsing into the small space offered.

Another man offered a bottle of water.

Juan Pablo barely managed a heartfelt gracias before he drank it all. Water had never tasted so sweet. Then, his head came to rest on bent knees.

As the truck took off, he knew a profound gratitude.

The men resumed their song.

Juan Pablo tried to think of a plan. If he could somehow get across the border again, he could find his way back to the shelter and hopefully be reunited with his violin. This was most urgent. But he could no longer involve anyone else in his struggle with this terrible man. To involve anyone put their lives at stake and he did not want to do that.

Even Rocio. Especially Rocio.

The sun was poised to set on the distant horizon. The air was still. The truck kicked up a cloud of dust behind it, obscuring the fast-receding landscape of uniform green. They at last turned down the wider lane leading off the farm.

"Javier, slow down," a man called out. "Juan Pablo, is this man driving a Cadillac?"

Juan Pablo looked up with alarm, but the men were already moving. A large wooden toolbox rested beneath the window of the truck's cab; it was lifted. Tools were withdrawn and one of the men motioned for him to get in. He fitted in. The lid shut. The truck had never stopped and the men, once again, resumed their song.

The men's boss stood in the road and waved them to a stop. Parked off at the side, the man with the red boots leaned against his Cadillac, smoking a cigar. He approached the truck to look in the truck bed.

Juan Pablo did not see this, but he didn't have to. Tense with renewed fear, he held his breath. He asked the Sky People for help.

"Some kid is hiding in the field."

"Ah, someone likes his zacate, sí? He is stealing from us, no?"

"He is wanted by the boss. There's a big reward if any of you work extra hours looking for the package."

"A reward?" Javier asked. "How much?"

"Five hundred pesos if you find him," the boss said.

Juan Pablo froze, afraid to breathe. He could not believe this sum. A month's worth of wages for working men.

"Help should be here any minute," the boss continued.

An animated conversation emerged from the men. Some wanted to help look, but one man reminded them that his wife was in labor and he needed to get back tonight. Another man had a beautiful woman waiting for him in Tijuana. No amount of money could induce him to stay, not even 500 pesos. This solicited warm teases and jealous catcalls from the other less fortunate men.

Meanwhile, the cigar-smoking man looked in the truck bed; his gaze went slowly from man to man. One of the men asked if he had an extra smoke. This was produced from a shirt pocket and handed over.

Ultimately, the men declined this generous offer.

The truck moved on.

Juan Pablo's relief, keenly and intensely felt, burst through his mind in a symphony. Not just any symphony, but his mother's and abuela's favorite one. He imagined holding his beloved violin; he harmonized every triumphant note of that transcendent music. He vowed to play it soon in Pacific Grove.

He had escaped.

CHAPTER SEVENTEEN

The symphony lasted until they reached Tijuana and he gave his heartfelt thanks to the men who had saved him. "He will not get you again," the old driver said.

"No. Never again," Juan Pablo repeated with feeling.

Darkness came slowly in the summer as Juan Pablo made his way through the side streets back to the border crossing. He was emotionally and physically spent; he had no thoughts beyond that he had escaped, that he was not to die today. At last he reached the freeway off-ramp. Facing the fast-moving lights, he walked toward the oncoming traffic until he found it.

Resting inconspicuously against the chainlink fence, amidst a river of litter, his backpack waited. He swept it up and began walking to the main boulevard. The turnoff put him ever closer to the border crossing. As he was about to leave the freeway, he stopped and stood for several moments noticing the people hawking wares at the border crossing on the other side of the freeway: trinkets, souvenirs, candy, even ponchos and purses and Levi's.

He could sell his milkweed seeds here.

It would be perfect. He would make enough money to eat while he discovered a means of crossing the border again.

He waited and watched the people. Most wore lighted, colorful hats as they weaved up and down the lanes. He looked across the endless stream of headlights. Stands packed with a colorful array of goods lined the freeway on one side.

He watched an older woman selling maracas and ridiculously large sombreros—these, he reasoned, must be decorative. Wearing a funny hat with blinking red and white lights, the short, squat woman moved slowly, indifferently, as if she had been there all her life.

He moved toward her, crossing two lanes of stopped traffic. "Pardon, señorita?"

The warmth in her smile surprised him. The bright and shining false teeth were incongruent with her lined face and heavy jowls, but she showed them off like a pleased child holding a carefully drawn self-portrait.

"I am looking for work," he first explained, after answering with his own smile. "I was wondering if you can tell me how I might work here, at the crossing."

Her eyes made a brief study of him. "Your eyes. Very pretty." She laughed. "They are wasted on a young man."

Juan Pablo smiled back; he supposed this was true.

"You remind me of my son Gabriel, God rest his soul, for no reason I can say. So," she changed tones with the subject, "you want to rent a lane?"

"Yes," he nodded.

The smile dropped. "This is no easy feat," she said, shifting the pile of ten straw sombreros to her other hand.

"Oh? Why is that?"

"A thousand people want to rent a lane," she exaggerated, but not by much. "When there is an opening, the man in charge has a list. People pay him just to be on this list of one hundred names. Even if you had the money, you would have to wait years."

Juan Pablo paused as a car honked its horn and she attended to the sale. He watched as a large hat disappeared inside a Buick and the money slipped into the pocket of her apron.

When she returned to his side, he asked, "Who is in charge of this list?"

"Felix. He controls the list and all vendors."

"Where can I find him?"

"He's often found at the Rancheros bar on Avenida Revolución. But you should not bother. He will turn you away."

"How did you get a spot?"

She laughed. "Felix is my other son. He better give his mother a spot!"

Then she moved on, walking in front of the waiting traffic.

Juan Pablo stood there, blinded by the sea of bright headlights. He would not give up so easily. There must be a way to get a spot. He chased after the old woman. "Uno momento, señorita."

Stopping, she waited for him to catch up.

"There must be some way, a secret way, to leap to the top of the list."

The old woman did not want to send him off with false hope, but somehow she could not resist answering.

The key, she explained as the cars moved slowly past them, came with a brief lesson in border-crossing economics. Over the decades, her son Felix (as had his father before him) experimented with selling every kind of trinket here; a list that included the top 100 bestselling items in a pharmacy. Over these long decades, they had discovered their bestselling items fell into one of two categories: *viejo como un anciano*, meaning Mexican souvenirs, wicker baskets, colorful clay pots, and cheap lanterns; or cheap cigarettes, candies, and gum.

"My son is a smart businessman." The dazzling smile showed up again as she explained this. "So, if say, you came up with something new, an item that he has not yet tried, something that was novel and cheap, something that caught his attention, he might give you a two-day slot. To see if it sells."

A heart-stopping look of happiness appeared on Juan Pablo's face; she might have just told him he won the lottery.

"Gracias, señorita. Gracias."

And he disappeared into the lights.

CHAPTER EIGHTEEN

A warm haze spread over the main avenue in Tijuana. Avenida Revolución. High-end stores competed with souvenir shops for the ever-dwindling tourist dollar. Homeless now, Juan Pablo spent the night with half a dozen other homeless kids behind a leather goods shop. In a group they headed to a church for food in the morning. They had to go early, as there was never enough for everyone. "Look sickly," a boy, Pedro, advised as they stood in line, "or the sisters will pick you out to work."

The sisters, though, took no notice of the swarms of young and old lining up outside the gate surrounding the modest church. Or so Juan Pablo thought. "You," a voice called from the church steps.

Everyone turned to look at him. A few of the other boys snickered at his poor luck.

"Me?" Juan Pablo pointed.

The sister nodded. "Can you help in the kitchen?"

Juan Pablo stepped forward. "I am happy to help."

The sisters smiled at him as he was led behind the church to the nearby rectory kitchen. The fair-sized room was made of wooden floors. A modest cross hung on the walls near the brick oven, which already warmed the room. Five sisters—all clad in traditional habits, but worn, thin ones—were busy over pots of oatmeal, loaves of cornbread, and bowls of jam. One of the sisters directed him to sit at their small table.

"And what is your name, young man?"

"Juan Pablo."

His name solicited warm smiles all around. Catholics always assumed he was named after the famous pope.

"Pope John Paul's favorite song is 'Pescador de Hombres.' Maybe it is yours too, Juan Pablo?"

Before he could answer, the sisters' voices rose in song.

Juan Pablo smiled as a giant bowl of oatmeal, a slice of cornbread, and water were set before him. One sister patted his shoulder before pouring a generous heaping of brown sugar serendipitously into his bowl. He tried to slow down, but he had never been this hungry or thankful for a simple meal. The sisters never spoke after that, beyond directing his labor, as there wasn't time.

Instead they sang or hummed as they worked and Juan Pablo was reminded how much music sustained people. In the next few hours over 200 hungry people were served a good breakfast. He spent the rest of the day scrubbing plates and pots and sweeping, all the while working out his plan. At last everything was done, ready for the sisters to begin a new day.

Then he was thanked, kissed, and sent away.

Once free, he spent two hours working on his sign.

Finally, as the day wore down, he found himself on Tijuana's infamous main boulevard. The Avenida Revolución used to be swarming with rich Americans on a brief shopping holiday. Now, due to the ever-ominous presence of the cartels, only the foolish or the brave made their way across the border just to shop. Fewer Americans came every week. The once glittering streets had fallen into disrepair, doors were shuttered and stores boarded over. Only a few bars serving working people were able to remain open.

Juan Pablo moved from the dwindling light of day into the darker cavern that was the Rancheros bar. Empty tables rested on a sawdust-covered floor. A thick cloud of smoke hung motionless in the air. A handful of men sat at the bar, beers and tequila shots placed in front of them like a uniform table setting.

"Excuse me," Juan Pablo said as he approached the bar.

The bartender, a small, compact man, looked over.

"I am looking for Felix."

"Ah. All the world is looking for Felix. He only sees people on Mondays."

The two men at the end of the bar held cards in their hands, emitting drunken laughter as they played blackjack. Two other young, strong-looking men sat between a heavyset man who spoke rapidly into a phone. No one gave him a moment's attention. One man watched the front door and the other kept his eyes on an open side door.

Juan Pablo guessed they were bodyguards for the heavy man in the middle.

"If you direct me to him, I would be very quick," Juan Pablo offered politely.

The bartender glanced at the heavyset man in the middle.

The man returned his phone to his trousers. "I'm not taking any new vendors, amigo," he replied. "Try again in a couple of months."

Juan Pablo found himself staring at the very large dark-haired man in between the two bodyguards. He had a long, black mustache and wore a large red and white Mexican poncho, the kind found in any tourist shop, the kind, in fact, sold at the border crossing. The colorful poncho draped over a white T-shirt and black jeans. His amused and intelligent eyes gave Juan Pablo a quick look-over.

"I believe I would be very successful."

"Ha. You and a thousand others."

"I would also take any time slot, señor. Even in the slow hours of night and early morning."

He grinned as he took a sip of beer. "There are no slow hours at the border."

Juan Pablo played his best card. "Your mother told me the key to gaining a spot as a vendor."

This received the man's full attention, and he chuckled. "What did the old lady tell you?"

"That to earn one of these coveted places, I must offer something special, something original. I believe I have it, señor."

"You have this miracle item? And it would be a wonder if it was not something I have not thought of and tried and dismissed. The only items that move at the border are the things already there: ponchos, trousers, purses, sombreros, candy, toys, dolls, you name it, if it sells, believe me, it's out there. I even have Chinese basura now—the only people on earth who can squeeze a peso from a poor Mexican."

"You don't have milkweed seeds to save the butterflies."

Juan Pablo held up his sign and presented a packet of seeds, wrapped neatly in his abuela's bright orange ribbon, as if it were a jeweled brooch of queens.

Felix's eyes surveyed the sign: MONARCH BUTTERFLY RESCUE PROJECT: MILKWEED SEEDS FOR THE GARDEN.

The men at the bar stopped talking and turned to stare.

Juan Pablo explained that people buy the seeds to help the butterflies on their journeys, that attracting butterflies to their garden excited all but the most hardened hearts. He promised the seeds would fly out of his hands.

No one contradicted the earnest young man.

Felix's gaze lifted from the simple allure of the packet to Juan Pablo's large green eyes, so full of hope. For some reason, Juan Pablo's eyes reminded him of his much-loved younger brother, God rest his soul, lost to him many years ago.

"How much do you think you can sell them for?"

"Twenty pesos a packet."

Felix took a long swig of his beer, set it down, and said, "I take half."

Juan Pablo nodded. "Gracias!"

196

Juan Pablo left as soon as Felix dispatched strict instructions. The men smiled as the boy disappeared to make his fortune. One of the men playing cards shook his head. The boy looked somehow familiar. Where had he seen him before?

CHAPTER NINETEEN

The young man selling milkweed seeds attracted a lot of attention from the endless stream of cars entering the United States from Mexico. Juan Pablo walked between cars in the steady stop-and-go traffic at the border. He held out his sign to each car. If they wanted a packet, they rolled down their window, and Juan Pablo was treated to a blast of cool air-conditioned air. Money and seeds were exchanged, "gracias" said, and he moved on to the next car. Occasionally, a car honked from another lane and he had to race to reach the customer.

The hot sun beat upon the black river of lanes, which reflected and intensified the heat. He wore a Giants baseball hat for protection, dark sunglasses, and a bright red T-shirt with Levi's—new clothes, so no one looking for him would recognize him. So far he had seen five black Cadillacs, and each sighting had sent his heart racing while he hid behind the stalls, but none had been the Hunter.

He had already made fifty-five American dollars, enough to pay Felix and buy a nice meal. The good Sisters of Mercy let him sleep in the kitchen in return for help in the predawn hours preparing for hungry hordes who gathered every day. His stomach clenched with a demand for attention; he was starving, he was always half-starving now. He needed to sell just three more packets for an even $60 before he took a break to feed his ever-complaining stomach.

He could not risk contacting Rocio, not yet. It was still too dangerous.

During his long nights alone in the small kitchen, he faced his problem. The man with the red boots was not giving up, he knew this. Not only would he have to find some way (somehow!) to cross

199

the border and enter California and make his way first to the shelter to get his violin back, and then find his way to Pacific Grove, but he could not involve anyone in the journey.

First, get his violin back or die trying.

Second, make his way to Pacific Grove.

He did not have a plan after this. Life seemed too tenuous, too uncertain. *Some lives are like a good novel: you never know what will happen until you turn the page.*

He would wait until the page was turned . . .

If he had the time or energy to worry about not having a plan after Pacific Grove, he might have wondered if his fate itself was going to stop there. Was the last page of his life Pacific Grove? He tried to convince himself that he still might have a future of music and Rocio and all their plans, but it all seemed distant, uncertain, and fuzzy now, like a long-ago memory or a dream upon waking.

No, not uncertain—he stopped, realizing, it seemed impossible.

And really none of this even mattered unless he found a way to cross the border. It was already late August. Time was running out. Every morning, in the predawn hours, he asked the Sky People for help, but so far, he was still without his violin or Rocio, running lanes on the wrong side of the border.

These were his thoughts the morning the warning buzz started softly, barely perceptible.

Juan Pablo kept looking to the border crossing as he worked. An ominous two-story-high metal fence ran across the whole of Tijuana. It started far out to sea and ended hundreds of miles past the city's border. Two or three armed guards manned every passage through. Cars drove up, the border agent looked in, exchanged a few words, examined documents, and then waved the car through. Occasionally, for no reason anyone knew, a car was singled out and motioned over for a more thorough examination.

A horn drew Juan Pablo's gaze to a shiny blue Prius, three lanes over. He rushed over. A dark window swept down, blasting him with the sweet relief of air conditioning. Two young and pretty Mexican ladies spoke at once.

"We love butterflies!"

"We'll take two packets," the other lady said from the passenger seat.

After handing them two packets, he collected the money and turned to another honking car several lanes over. As he rushed over to the silver Honda, he became fully conscious of the buzzing sound. He looked across the lanes of stop-and-go traffic until he spotted the black Cadillac.

His body mobilized for flight as he ducked around the cars, keeping his back to the oncoming danger. It was maybe twenty cars away. Was it him?

He didn't know, didn't know how he could know, but he couldn't take any chances. He started back across the lanes of traffic.

A brand-new red Mercedes rolled down its window.

"Hello?" A friendly American voice shouted to him. "How much for the seeds?"

Stalling, trying to think of what to do and where to hide, Juan Pablo headed to the car. The back-seat windows rolled down to reveal two kids. Just as he was about to hand them the seeds, the girl screamed, "Oh! A butterfly! Look!"

Juan Pablo turned to see a giant monarch floating above the stalled traffic. His thoughts tumbled in confusion. As he turned around, a little dog jumped from the window.

"Kipper! Kipper! Catch him!"

"Ohmygod, he's going to get run over!"

The little dog chased after the butterfly.

Juan Pablo sprinted after the dog.

The lady got out of the car just as the traffic started moving forward. Horns honked behind her. She stopped, turned around, and jumped back into the car to move it forward.

Juan Pablo kept running. "Stop! Stop!"

The little guy ran right beneath the butterfly, leaping up. The dog was an impressive jumper. The butterfly flitted on, unmindful of the commotion. The butterfly and the dog headed straight toward the border crossing.

Juan Pablo didn't realize what was happening at first. He meant only to catch little Kipper before a car hit it. He was about twenty paces behind the dog, closing in.

The butterfly disappeared from sight. The dog kept running.

"Catch him," he called out to the border guards.

Unable to hear above the background noise, the border guards bent over to inspect a car. Kipper rushed right on through and into America.

And, in the split second, Juan Pablo grasped the whole situation.

"Kipper!" he called as if the dog belonged to him. "Kipper!"

The boy followed the dog right though the underpass, past the two border guards, side-stepping the dropped gate, and continuing to chase after the dog. He knew they would not shoot a boy trying to catch his dog.

Juan Pablo only knew to keep running after Kipper. The guards might give chase, but they would not shoot. He never once looked back. A strange and magical exhilaration filled him with each step.

From a great distance he heard, "Whoa! Stop! Hey, hey! You can't cross the border! You . . . Stop!"

Kipper ran onto the overpass leading right to the walkway in America.

Juan Pablo just kept running and running. He never did look back.

The dog stopped on the freeway off-ramp.

"Kipper, Kipper," Juan Pablo knelt down, exhilarated and relieved.

Wagging his tail, looking for all the world contrite, Kipper came to Juan Pablo. He swept the little dog safely into his arms. Holding him, he looked back over the border. No one and nothing rushed at him. Kipper's car had reached the border crossing. The driver spotted him and flashed the car lights. The Mercedes pulled onto the side of the ramp.

A girl flew out of the car. "Kipper!"

Juan Pablo handed the little guy to the girl.

"You saved him! Thank you, thank you." She took the unrepentant dog into her arms.

Relief and happiness mixed on her face. The girl had long, tangled blonde hair and gray eyes. She wore shorts and a sleeveless red top over her stick-thin form.

Her father came out of the car, too. "Thank you so much. That was very brave. If something happened to Kipper, Amelie wouldn't survive. Or Zack." He removed a wad of cash. "Can I give you a reward?"

The cash made him draw back with surprise. "No, no. It was my pleasure." He stopped himself from explaining how he should be paying them. After all, he was standing in America. He made it.

Juan Pablo had trouble grasping this lucky turn of events. Luck that involved a dog and a butterfly that came just as he was losing all hope, and that might very well have come just in time.

It was just two or three hours to Ventura where, hopefully, he could get his violin back.

"There must be something we can do for you," the girl's father said.

Amelie and the man looked alike, but the father looked too young. Sunglasses sat atop his shaved head. He had kind eyes and wide lips, lifted in a beguiling smile. Did he know he had just crossed the border illegally? His smile suggested he did, as if it were their secret.

Juan Pablo turned briefly away from the man to the border, where in minutes a black Cadillac would be crossing into the United States. He did need to escape. He had $60. "Could you be so kind as to drop me off at the bus stop? It is just a few blocks from here."

"The bus stop?" the man questioned, as if he were unfamiliar with the idea of buses. "Where are you going?"

"I need to pick up my violin in Ventura."

"Oh. You're a musician." This too was said mysteriously, as if now everything made sense.

Juan Pablo nodded. "Yes," he said.

"What the heck is your violin doing in Ventura? Never mind," he said before Juan Pablo could answer, smiling again. "We're headed home to Santa Barbara. Why don't we give you a lift all the way?"

You will notice, Juan Pablo, people will appear in your life at the exact right moment. They are acting for the Sky People to help you.

Do they know this, Abuela? That they are acting for the Sky People?

Almost never.

Then how do you know they are sent by the Sky People?

Because the luck is such that it can only be understood as a miracle.

Abuela, he had laughed, *the Sky People always seem too fantastic to be real.*

Yes, she agreed. *That is why many people do not recognize their gifts.*

"Thank you. That would be . . . amazing," was all Juan Pablo could say.

Just like that, he found himself inside a bright red Mercedes, seated between Amelie and her brother, Zack, who looked like a masculine, older version of his sister. As the Mercedes circled the on-ramp and found the way back to the freeway, Juan Pablo gave silent thanks to the butterfly, to little Kipper, to the Sky People. He caught the father's enigmatic smile in the review mirror.

Juan Pablo smiled back. He was on his way to reclaim his violin.

"You play the violin?" Zack asked. "Cool . . ."

CHAPTER TWENTY

The red Mercedes pulled up to the curb in front of Port Hueneme. After saying his goodbyes to Amelie, Zack, and Kipper, wanting to cry from all his gratitude for their help, Juan Pablo got out. He waved as the car drove away. He turned to the familiar building, dark now behind the high wire gate. He prayed his violin was still here in the storage room.

He remembered the night guard, a nice man who hopefully would remember him as well. He approached the guard house and peered inside. Arms folded over his ample belly, Mr. Hall sat slumped in his chair, eyes closed, sound asleep.

Juan Pablo saw no reason to wake him. He slipped around the barrier and headed toward the doors. He stepped quietly inside. He knew that everyone would be asleep except for the other night security guard and the nurse on night duty. They usually watched TV in the administration office.

The office was the first door on the left. Making no sound, he crept forward. The door was open. The night watchman and the nurse watched a police show, their backs to the door. Juan Pablo tiptoed past and continued down the hall to the back of the building. He passed two dorm rooms where the children slept. Standing on tiptoes, he peered through the small square window near the top. Empty. Neat rows of empty bunks on each side of the room.

The door to the other dorm remained open. He cautiously looked inside. This was half full. Girls slept on one side of the room, boys on the other. Only one girl slept on the top bunk. Everyone was asleep, it seemed.

He found the storage room, but it was locked.

He knew where a key was kept.

He quietly made his way back down the hall to Dolores's office. This was unlocked. He stepped inside the familiar space. A flick of a switch brought bright light over the desk and computer. He opened the top drawer.

There it sat, waiting for him.

Grabbing it, he started back out when something caught his attention. A Post-it note stuck to Dolores's computer. Written in neat letters: *Dr. Juan Laves? Dr. John Keys of Stanford University?*

The buzzing started in his ears.

For several long minutes he just stared at the obvious explanation of a lifelong mystery. His abuela said his father's name was Dr. Juan Laves, but his abuela translated the name to Spanish. His father was an American. He had assumed he was Mexican American and he had searched for Dr. Juan Laves.

Of course he would have an American name. Dr. Juan Laves was Dr. John Keys. Dolores had guessed the simple translation of mixed languages.

Not once had he ever thought to translate the name to English.

In an instant he knew what he would do: collect his violin, find Dr. John Keys at Stanford University, contact him, and if he was interested, if he really was his father, they would arrange a meeting.

He knew exactly where he would arrange the meeting.

He'd write a note to Dolores and Rocio telling them not to worry, that he'd contact them after he reached Pacific Grove.

Heart racing with a previously unknown kind of excitement, Juan Pablo grabbed the keys and made his way to the storage room. As soon as the door opened, he didn't even bother turning on the lights. He saw across the distance. His violin waited on top of the lockers.

In the next minute it was in his hands.

Tears filled his eyes. Tears of relief and joy.

He vowed it would never leave his hands again.

His reprieve was a physical force and a powerful one. He resisted the urge to open it and start playing for all his joy. The last thing he wanted now was attention.

He spotted his iPad resting on a shelf nearby.

He turned it on and immediately discovered Rocio's texts.

He scrolled to the top, to read them in order.

JP, we are so worried. I cannot eat or sleep. No one knows where you are, what has become of you. Dolores called us . . . What is the English word that mixes hysteria with fear and panic? Oh, if you were here you would tell me!

Juan Pablo supplied the word in his mind: *frantic.*

Dolores said you had been taken to an orphanage in Mexico by mistake, but when she called the orphanage listed on your paperwork, they have no knowledge of you. Then Dolores couldn't find the bus that had taken you. We are calling every orphanage in Mexico, but there are so many and most do not have phones. There are only Internet connections and no one answers our pleas.
We don't know what to do. We don't know where you are.
I finally told my mom what happened, what really happened, the whole thing. The man with the red boots. She is crazy with worry now too, afraid he has got you.
Juan Pablo! Find your way back to us!
Now the police in Mexico are involved and the police in CA. There are alerts for you. Everyone is looking. Dolores hired a private detective team.
I have so much to tell you!
Juan Pablo, Elena did a terrible thing. Dolores has found your father, your real father. His name is Dr. John Keys. He is the nicest

man alive, I think, a professor of biology at Stanford University in California. He specializes in the migration of animals and wrote a book about the migration of butterflies and he married your mom in the church in Guadalajara! The same one we pretended to get married in, remember? Elena told him you had died with your mom. My mother says we must forgive Elena, that she couldn't bear losing you after your mom died, she just couldn't and because he was an American, she was afraid he would take you away from her. She always told my mom that your father abandoned you to her and because so many men do this, she never questioned it.

Since this news, your father has called my mom many times. I got to talk to him for a long time. He wanted to know everything about you. Juan Pablo it made him, a grown man, a professor, cry. Dolores has talked to him many times, too.

Now, like all of us, his heart is sick with worry.

Call us, Juan Pablo.

I love you, Juan Pablo.

Juan Pablo read this three times. He tried to make sense of it, of the idea that his abuela had kept him away from his father all these years. Could it be true? Could his abuela have done such a thing?

The idea of his abuela lying seemed as impossible as the sun rising in the west. She just wouldn't, couldn't, never had, never would. And yet . . .

She had lied to him and it had not been a small lie.

All his life he had known how much his abuela loved his mother; she had told him a thousand times. *Juan Pablo, your beautiful mother played that piece. I remember it well. She was sitting right there, too, wearing shorts and a red T-shirt.*

Your mother used to play in the meadow, too, every day.

This was my favorite piece your mother played.

That is just what your mother said when she saw The Sound of Music *for the first time.*

I remember the first time I took Julieta to Mexico City to hear the symphony

One time: *I thought I understood death and loss and grief, but*—she had shaken her head—*if not for you, Juan Pablo, I could not have borne the loss of your mother. You are my sun now.*

Juan Pablo sat up straight in the darkened storage room, illuminated now by the light of his iPad. The warning buzz sounded loud in his ears as he considered this, the terrible idea of what his abuela had done. Not to him. He had known only love from his abuela. She had given him everything a person could want: his music, a good education, books, Rocio, his love of the butterflies. No, her crime had been committed against his father, his real father.

She had stolen a son from his father.

Oh, Abuela! How could you?

He tried to think this through, to reason it out. She had so loved his mother, her only child, a bright and shining star. She had been accepted at such a young age as an apprentice to Mexico's National Symphony Orchestra. *Your mother, Juan Pablo, there was so much life in her. She was so beautiful.* Then she died to give him life.

As his thoughts spun over this information, he felt he brushed against understanding. His mother's baby, her grandson, how could she hand him over to another? To a man who would take him not just a thousand more kilometers away, but into another country. A foreign country.

A light blinking interrupted his thoughts and he looked down. A voice mail had just come in.

He clicked it on and Rocio's voice filled the silence:

"Juan Pablo, listen to me," Rocio's voice sounded into the darkened room.

Juan Pablo straightened, alerted by the fear in her voice. Something terrible had happened.

Whispers, pleas, static, and then:

"They are here! The men chasing us. We were eating dinner by the phone, always by the phone, waiting for your call and suddenly they were here. In the apartment! They hurt my mom, knocked her unconscious. She's lying in the bed. I am staring at their gun as I speak—no, no—"

"Twenty-four hours to contact this number with the location where to find you."

Click.

Pure adrenaline shot through Juan Pablo. His heart began a slow, steady escalation. The buzzing grew as loud as a full symphony heard from the front row.

He was facing the finale. This was it. The end.

All of life seemed the cruelest joke.

First his mother died when he was born.

Then his abuela stole him from his father.

Finally, on her deathbed, his abuela told him to follow the path of the butterflies to sanctuary at Pacific Grove, California. Here, she promised him, someone would be waiting for him.

All this time he had thought it would be someone who would rescue him. Like his father. Or Dolores. But it wasn't.

It turned out the person waiting for him would be the man with the red boots. The man who would end his life or Rocio's or both. The Hunter would be a harsh and ugly crescendo on an otherwise beautiful symphony that was his life.

He had learned he could accept his death, but he could never accept Rocio's.

He sat in the darkened room trying to think of what to do, but he couldn't come up with a way to change the ending. He wanted a happy ending.

Any happy ending meant Rocio was saved.

He had to save Rocio. Always, he had to save Rocio.

He texted back: *I will be at the butterfly sanctuary in Pacific Grove tomorrow before sunset.*

Ask the Sky People!

I love you with all my heart, Rocio.

He hit send.

There; it was done.

As he grabbed his violin and stuffed his iPad into his backpack, he asked the Sky People for help one last time. Not for him. He was doomed, he saw that now, but help for Rocio.

To that end he knew he had to make his way to the butterfly sanctuary.

At what point did he realize the Sky People were helping?

By the third car that stopped to give him a ride on his journey north.

The gray Ford SUV looked normal as it pulled over on the northbound Pacific Coast Highway off-ramp. Feeling dazed, numb even, going through the motions, Juan Pablo looked into the passenger window as the driver, an older man, leaned over. A blue baseball cap topped his gray hair, a thick mustache sat atop a mischievous smile. "Hey, partner," he said, his voice warm and friendly. "Where you headed?"

"Pacific Grove." He said the words like a question.

"Ha! Now there's a coincidence. That's right where I'm headed."

His abuela said there was no such thing as a coincidence.

"If you don't mind my sidekick, hop in."

Sidekick? Juan Pablo knew no translation. The great wonder of English was its millions of words. Words for every imaginable thing in the world and many things he had never imagined and would never have imagined until he heard the word.

Enlightenment came as he opened the door and he was greeted by a hundred or so pounds of a furry, blond dog. A warm tongue brushed the side of his face and despite every worry, Juan Pablo found himself smiling at the goofiest, friendliest dog in the world.

"Meet Kipper," the man said as the car pulled onto the freeway.

"Ah, your sidekick?" Juan Pablo asked as his hands greeted the sociable creature.

Sidekick meant a companion dog.

"Is that a violin?"

"Yes."

"You any good?"

"I try." Juan Pablo only pretended to be modest.

As he drove onto the freeway heading north, they exchanged names. The man introduced himself as Bill. "So where are you from, Juan Pablo?"

"El Rosario, Mexico's monarch butterfly sanctuary."

"Wow! Butterflies. My wife loved butterflies. She was always planting, what is it, those seeds . . ."

"Milkweed seeds?" Juan Pablo finally stopped petting his new friend, who now covered the entire back seat. He stared intently at the man.

"Yes. She was always planting those, you know, to attract the migrating butterflies."

Another coincidence. Juan Pablo felt a strange tingling on his forehead.

"She passed away recently," Bill said, his voice changing and looking distantly ahead. "Married forty-five years, two kids, grandkids, the works. To tell you the truth, I'm kind of lost without her. Kind of?" He questioned his own words before shaking his head. "I am seriously lost without her."

Studying the man, trying to make sense of all he was feeling, Juan Pablo touched his sadness, apparent in every word. "I am sorry for your loss," he replied softly. "It is a very hard thing to lose someone you love."

This received Bill's full attention. "You sound like you know from experience," he said.

He nodded. "I recently lost my grandmother who raised me," Juan Pablo said.

The silence filled with a revisiting of loves lost.

"Well, look at us," Bill broke the spell with a chuckle. "Aren't we a pair?"

Juan Pablo felt on the verge of tears. Crying would do no good, he told himself. He wisely thought to change the subject. His abuela always told him to ask people about their work, that whether it was good work or bad, people never realized how much adults liked to share this important part of their lives.

"What kind of work do you do?"

"Retired cop," he said. "I still do security consulting," he added, making quotation marks in the air around the word. Juan Pablo had seen this gesture in movies; it meant there was something pretend in the sentence, but he was not thinking of this now. For his next thought startled him.

Bill launched into an explanation of the security work, mostly for very rich people. He could write a book about the 1 percent and anyone who thought millions made one happy was dreaming . . .

Juan Pablo no longer listened because in the moment Bill said he was a retired cop, he understood what was happening. The loud and clear message that was being sent to him. He had been hitchhiking since early morning. He had caught three rides and all were from policemen: The first man was a Laguna Beach policeman who was picking up his daughter at the University of California–Santa Barbara, where she was a student. The second ride was from a military policeman on his way back to his base in northern California. And now Bill, the retired policeman who had just lost his wife who happened to love butterflies.

There is no such thing as coincidences, his abuela said a thousand times.

CHAPTER TWENTY-ONE

Rocio couldn't believe this was happening; she just couldn't.

Anxiety piled up in Rocio's mind as she sat with the two armed banditos. That Juan Pablo would be killed. Her mother would be killed. She would be killed.

Her head was about to explode.

She tried to think of how to escape.

She clasped her hands tightly, as if praying, but it was no prayer, all desperation.

Yet, without any real awareness, she sent a frantic prayer to Elena's Sky People.

"Will you really let us go once he has Juan Pablo?"

"Shut. Up," the tall one who had hit her mother said without even bothering to look at her. He wore Levi's, boots, and a jean vest over a black T-shirt, even though it was about a hundred degrees outside. His gun rested on his leg as they waited. He looked about thirty, tall, thin, and nondescript, except for a missing index finger and a scar that crossed his high cheekbone. He smelled faintly of rotting meat and flowery cologne, all mixed up.

"Shhh," the other man said, adding a terrifying smile. He, too, wore Levi's, along with a loose white T-shirt beneath a leather vest. He had a shaven head and a tattoo on his neck that said "rebel," but because he was overweight, even obese, the first two letters folded on themselves and appeared to read "feeble." *Feeble*, the English word for "dimwitted." Juan Pablo would have found it hilarious. This man, too, was missing an index finger. His gun rested on the coffee table, next to a glass of water. She kept staring at it, imagining picking it up in a flurry of bravery and turning the table on them.

How did they find two men, both with missing fingers?

The answer did not seem worth dwelling on.

They said nothing else to her, as if she were invisible.

She tried to determine if they were even watching the old movie. *The Untouchables*. Their faces never changed, whether someone was shot or saved. They just stared blankly at the screen.

They both looked crazily out of place in her mom's warm and colorful American apartment. Since arriving here, she dreamed of the day she would show Juan Pablo the grounds: the swimming pool, the manicured lawns, and the tropical landscape kept alive by a near-constant mist spraying over them, like a fairy tale, only real. There was also the empty "club house," a huge lodge with a couch and chairs, a TV, and a pool table. And the movie theaters!

Oh, Juan Pablo would love this place.

Now she would never see the amazement on his face.

She felt a prick of fury . . .

She studied the culprits. Perched casually on the pale lavender couch and chair respectively, their black boots looked foreign, out of place on the wood floors. The plan, they said, was to hold her until the Hunter had Juan Pablo, then they would leave.

What if her mother was bleeding in her brain? She could die!

But worse, they would only go once Juan Pablo was shot.

She had to do something.

"Sky People, help me."

Ridiculously, she said the words out loud.

"Geezus. I said shut the fuck up."

Rocio jerked at the harsh rebuke.

The doorbell rang.

Rocio almost screamed, but instantly the tall man aimed his gun at her and motioned for silence. The two men exchanged alarmed looks. The other picked up his gun up from the table and held it.

A loud knock followed. "Pizza delivery!"

Pizza delivery? Confused but not, Rocio thought of the Sky People rescuing her, and she improvised. "Our regular pizza guy," she whispered to the armed man, wondering if they were that stupid. "Saturday treat."

He exchanged glances with his cohort in crime and then nodded. Grabbing her arm, he lifted her up and moved to the door, gun aimed at her head.

They were in fact that stupid.

Rocio opened the door. She took one look at the hallway full of police wearing SWAT vests, even as a strong arm threw her into the hallway to safety.

At the exact moment gunfire exploded across the room.

CHAPTER TWENTY-TWO

The Hunter lit a cigar as he waited on the bench in the Monarch Butterfly Sanctuary in Pacific Grove. Towering eucalyptus trees on one side and sky-high pines on the other. No butterflies in the famous mists of central California, but it burned off by the afternoon and the ubiquitous California sunshine appeared on cue.

The moist air filled with the scent of pine and the ocean nearby.

Not a winged creature in sight.

Or any other creature. The park was deserted in the foggy afternoon.

He ignored all this; indeed, he was barely aware of his surroundings. He struggled several seconds to get a match lit in the drizzle, finally exhaling a fine plume of smoke that disappeared into the fog blanketing the coast. He dropped the match, noticing briefly the grass straining to grow between the pine needle–covered floor, struggling, like all of life, for a brief moment in the sun.

He returned to trying to decide if he should deliver the kid alive or just deliver the body. The bigger payout meant keeping him alive. But this was not a normal kid. He did not often exercise mercy, but he supposed he would now. The kid had escaped more than once. The young man deserved some measure of respect. He would kill him on the spot. Spare him the absurd barbarity of the torture that awaited him if he were to be delivered alive.

Besides, he didn't need the money.

He texted the message to kill the girl and her mother.

A helicopter overhead interrupted the stillness of the afternoon.

The very stillness alerted him. It was too still.

The Hunter reached for his gun, even as his gaze darted to the side where he noticed movement. Before he came to his feet he was surrounded by twenty armed men. He almost laughed at the irony of him, the celebrated Hunter being taken out by the slim, dark-haired kid, a nobody, *un don nadie*.

Before he managed to fire a shot, he felt what he had always been waiting for.

The rain of bullets that signaled the end.

CHAPTER TWENTY-THREE

Juan Pablo arrived early at the butterfly sanctuary.

The police had reunited him with Dolores and he had been staying with her lively family until their first meeting could be arranged. Only Dolores understood that it had to be here.

He would have liked to have Rocio here too, but she was at her mother's bedside in the hospital while her mother recovered from the concussion. Rocio would not leave her. It didn't matter. Rocio's and his fates were entwined, like twin planets circling a star; the music of their lives was forever linked.

He said goodbye to Dolores, Bill, and Kipper in the car. As soon as he had told Bill of all that had happened to him, the older man went into action. The police and FBI were called. In America the police still caught the bad guys, Bill was happy to explain. In fact the police enjoyed nothing more than stopping the bad guys.

He would not be returning with Dolores or Bill. It turned out that Dolores's daughter-in-law, Lisa, also a Stanford professor, knew his father. They had met six months ago at a faculty meeting. Because his father was understandably attracted to female musicians, and they had both been widowed, they had begun seeing each other before any connection to his life had occurred.

A coincidence? Juan Pablo found it hard to believe in such things these days. Did his abuela plan for him to save the whale and pull the padre back to the living after he delivered Rocio safely to her mother in America? Did she intend for him to end the life of a man wanted in two countries, a man responsible for over fifty deaths that the FBI knew of, a man on their most-wanted list? Or, did his abuela merely plan for him to meet his missing father in the butterfly sanctuary in Pacific Grove?

Save a life and slay a beast . . .

Was this happy ending orchestrated by the old woman, in the same way a composer writes the finest symphony?

He had talked to the man who was his father last night.

John had shared his abuela's only letter to him, delivered just after her death:

John:

I will not apologize for what I have done to you. I never had a choice. As soon as I held Juan Pablo in my arms, trying to see him through my tears, I knew I held my heart. I had his love for the last years of my life; I have no regrets.

You will have him for the rest of yours.

You will find him at the butterfly sanctuary in Pacific Grove in late August.

Elena

And so it came to pass.

As Juan Pablo stood beneath the towering eucalyptus trees and the windblown pines of Pacific Grove's butterfly sanctuary, he looked up, hoping to see a butterfly. There were none, but in the moment, none were needed. Patches of blue sky promised afternoon sunshine and maybe then, he thought, the butterflies would manifest and circle his music as they always had in faraway El Rosario.

He finally removed his violin from its case.

Bow in hand, he chose his mother's, his abuela's, and coincidentally, his father's favorite piece of music.

With love and tenderness, he positioned his familiar friend. Bow in hand, he began playing.

The distant sound of the haunting violin music floated through the trees and the tall man started running until he came across him, like a vision, in the middle of the grove. He stopped, transfixed by his first sight of him, Juan Pablo, his son. The tall, slender, dark-haired youth stood in the stream of sunlight falling through the trees, lost to the music he created. A butterfly circled overhead as if he needed more proof of the miracle.

Juan Pablo spotted the tall man coming toward him and felt the recognition. It was the recognition of two souls finding each other at long last. Still, until the end, he continued playing the beautiful music.

Beethoven's "Ode to Joy."

For his mother, for his abuela, for all the Sky People listening . . .